I0563668

Unbreakable

Book One in the "Casts of Silver" Series

K.J. ROWE

Ark House Press
PO Box 1722, Port Orchard, WA 98366 USA
PO Box 1321, Mona Vale NSW 1660 Australia
PO Box 318 334, West Harbour, Auckland 0661 New Zealand
arkhousepress.com

"Unbreakable" Copyright © 2021 by K.J. Rowe.

All rights reserved. No part of this book may be reproduced in any form or by any electronic or mechanical means including information storage and retrieval systems, without permission in writing from the author. The only exception is by a reviewer, who may quote short excerpts in a review.

Unless otherwise stated all Scriptures are taken from THE HOLY BIBLE, NEW INTERNATIONAL VERSION®, NIV® Copyright © 1973, 1978, 1984, 2011 by Biblica, Inc.® Used by permission. All rights reserved worldwide.

Edited by Michele Pollock Dalton

This book is a work of fiction. Names, characters, places, and incidents either are products of the author's imagination or are used fictitiously. Any resemblance to actual persons, living or dead, events, or locales is entirely coincidental.

Cataloguing in Publication Data:
Title: Unbreakable
ISBN: 978-0-6451080-8-8 (pbk)
Subjects: Fiction
Other Authors/Contributors: Rowe, K.J.

Design by initiateagency.com

"But He said to me: My grace is sufficient for you, for My power is made perfect in weakness…"
2 Corinthians 12:9 NIV

ONE

There was only one thing that Lexi Slaydon disliked more than her brother's sarcasm, and that was being the center of attention. Assured chair races would be a fun way to close the evening at youth group, Lexi positioned herself on the office chair and pulled the helmet on; her unconvinced gaze square on her teammate, Nick Marshal. As the teams lined up and the cheers of spectators in the hall grew increasingly louder, the last thing Lexi saw was the grin on Nick's face as he shut her helmet's visor. The race started with a sudden thrust, and with a yelp of surprise, Lexi drew her legs up into her chest, causing the chair to wobble. "Put your legs down," Nick hissed against the helmet. "You'll tip us over!"

"This is not a fun game, Nick!" Lexi shouted back, feeling her stomach drop and head swim with each spin, thrust, stop, and jolt of the race. Though she knew the logic of his order, fear kept her clinging to the chair in a tight ball while mentally placing chair races at the top of her "dislikes" list. "Lexi! Legs!"

Reflex overthrew fear at Nick's shout, and Lexi threw her legs down with force. Her eyes flew open. And Lexi realized what a mistake she'd made - seeing the room begin to tilt. Closing her eyes again, she braced for impact. The hardwood floor greeted her side hard, forcing the wind from her lungs and jarring her shoulder, moments before the chair tumbled over her. Gasps echoed close by while distant shouts and cheers continued on. Once freed from under the chair, Lexi pushed the helmet off her head and caught sight of Nick sprawled on the floor next to her. He returned her gaze through the legs of those offering to help them up, and she proffered a weak smile.

Nick's grey eyes softened as he pushed himself up. Then he offered a hand to Lexi. In an effort to restore some semblance of dignity, she brushed her hair back from her face and took his hand - just as the other team crossed the finish line. "Ahem . . ."

Lexi rested her hands on her hips and glanced at Nick. She knew his competitive side well, and he wouldn't be impressed she'd lost the race for them. "Yeah, um, sorry about that."

He laughed, "Sorry's not going to cut it, girl! A lot was riding on that race."

As the next teams lined up at the start line, Lexi rolled her eyes and stretched out her arm - feeling her shoulder begin to tighten. "Of course there was, Nick. What was it? A five-buck bet with Dylan? Anyway, think I'll go see if Carla wants a hand in the kitchen. I'm not hanging around here to get roped into that again."

"Ah, I wouldn't worry, Lexi. Don't think anyone would ask you if you did." Open mouthed, Lexi turned to Nick, catching his teasing sideways glance at her.

"Just joking," he chuckled. "And it was ten dollars!"

With a deliberate move, Lexi shoved Nick with her shoulder as she turned. Then she made her way through the young people to the rear of the hall where the kitchen was. From the security of the fixed bar stool, Lexi watched the games continue. While the idea of chair races had received the vote for the end of the night game, she had felt uncomfortable with the idea. Lexi knew it would end up in tears. So, she had offered to help Carla prepare the youth café. However, her friends wanted nothing to do with that idea. In the end, humiliation showed up, along with an injury. She rubbed her shoulder once more and pushed the memory of concerned faces from her mind. She hated being embarrassed!

"Hey girl, you're here early. What can I get you?"

Lexi smiled as Carla's melodic voice chimed into her thoughts, grateful for the distraction. "Just a tea thanks."

"I really don't need to ask, do I?" Carla said with lightness. "Love that red you've put in your hair by the way."

"Thanks," Lexi said, straightening in her seat. "Hey, do you need a hand back there?"

Carla shook her head in reply as she returned to the kitchen. As the doors swung closed behind her, Lexi turned back to watch the games unfold when she locked eyes with Hope - one of her best friends.

Hope Meyer had joined The Valley Youth Group with Lexi almost seven years ago when they were just fourteen years old, and they had become inseparable since. With her feisty attitude, savvy smarts, and shaggy blond bob, Hope wasn't afraid to dive into anything – a trait Lexi often wished she had. So, as Hope stood by the side of the hall waving her over, Lexi shook her head. She was not joining in that game again. However, catching Hope then slip from the room through the side door, Lexi craned her neck after her. Where was she going?

"Here you go, sweetie. One tea," Carla said, placing a steaming mug on the table before her. "And a little choccie. I saw that tumble from the chair."

Lexi huffed and reached for the chocolate. "Thanks, Carla."

"Lexi, can I borrow you for a moment?" Dave said, appearing beside her just as she popped the chocolate in her mouth. Dave Thomas, The Valley's youth minister, was a force to be reckoned with. Whether it was because he was American or because of his energetic nature, people were drawn to him.

"Just let her take her tea with her, Dave," Carla said, before turning back to the kitchen.

A question tickled Lexi's features as she looked between the two before giving Dave a quick nod. When he gestured for her to follow him and left the hall at pace, Lexi scooped up her tea and followed - hurriedly chewing the chocolate as she went. Moments later, Lexi followed her Youth Minister into his quiet church office - surprised to find four of her friends already reclining lazily around the room. Including Hope and Nick. Though she'd never entered a lion's den before, she sensed it would feel somewhat similar as she tucked a leg under herself and sat down on the plaid sofa next to Dylan Saunders. While Dave organized notes on his desk, Lexi cradled the mug between her hands and leaned over to Dylan. "Hey, what's going on?"

He shrugged, his voice hushed. "I'm sure we'll find out soon enough. Nasty fall in the game, by the way, you alright?"

She took a sip of her tea, "Yeah, I'm fine. Who won?"

"Trent and his teammate, Sophie."

Trent Vaughan, the dark horse of the group. Quiet and unassuming, Trent seemed to come out with talents every now and then that surprised them. When Trent turned to her, Lexi lifted her mug to him. He dipped his head in acknowledgment.

Dave's office was always calming to Lexi, with its motivational prints and scripture verse artwork - not to mention it often smelt like freshly baked bread. But today, there was a different feeling in the air. Anticipation? As Dave cleared his throat, Lexi took another sip of tea, as a little butterfly fluttered in her stomach. "Ok, all," he said. "I'll make this quick. As you know, Carla and Mark are leaving us in three weeks for this year's mission trip, and we need new youth leaders. We've grown over the last couple of years. So, keeping to the Safe Ministry guidelines of one leader for every ten children, I need five new leaders."

The realization of why she had been called to the office dawned, and Lexi went cold. Lowering her mug, she swallowed hard.

"Is this your round-about way of asking us to step up?" Hope said, her cheerful upward inflection breaking the silence that had fallen over the room. Hope straightened in her seat like a soldier to attention. Dave nodded, and Hope's smile doubled in brilliance. "Oh! This is going to be so great."

"Mark, Carla, and I have managed well over the years – with the help of some volunteers from time to time," Dave continued. "But I need to reform the structure of the group if it's going to continue to run well."

Looking around the small office, Lexi could see that it wasn't just Hope that thought Dave's idea was great. Dylan had already angled toward Nick and Trent, who were perched on stools at the edge of Dave's desk. Mouth dry, Lexi took another sip of her tea as painful flashbacks of high school presentations flickered in her mind. She was bright, bubbly, and every bit as animated as Hope; however only comfortable being so within her own network of family and friends. What Dave was proposing would put her front and center each week before the toughest of critics – teenagers and young adults.

"Lexi?"

"Yeah?" Lexi asked, sensing that she'd tuned out an important part of the conversation while lost in thought. After batting away a paper ball Nick playfully threw at her, Lexi repositioned herself on the couch.

Dave cleared his throat. "Are you in, Lexi? Would you like to be part of the new Leadership Team?"

Her mind stuck on the word 'lead.' Conflicted, Lexi looked at each of her friends as they looked back at her; waiting for her answer. In this room, with these people, she felt safe and confident, but it would be a whole other story in front of a room full of young people. Her heart thumped within her chest, and she moistened her lips, thinking over what it would be like to lead the Friday night youth program. Excitement and fear tickled her mind. If she wanted to keep pursuing a career as a youth worker, she'd have to push through her fears eventually. Maybe. "Ok," she answered impulsively. "Ok, yeah. Thanks, Dave."

Catching glances of encouragement from her friends, Lexi absently listened to Dave wrapping up the meeting. But she remained distracted. What if part of the role required her to speak in front of audiences and she couldn't do it? What if she froze, or worse case, passed out? The last thought made her cringe, and Lexi shuddered when laughter drew her back to reality. Masking the confusion she felt with a smile, Lexi took the slip of paper Dave handed her and joined the others as they filed out of the office. While her friends talked excitedly about the meeting, Lexi speared off and headed to the empty kitchen to rinse out her mug. From the kitchen serving window, she watched Carla and Mark wrapping up the evening. Then, remembering the piece of paper Dave gave her, she pulled it out to read the message within. *Leadership Team meeting. My place, Monday nights. 7:00 p.m. Dave.* With a sigh, Lexi folded the piece of paper and slid it into the back pocket of her jeans. "Here we go."

TWO

"Hey, sis!"

The familiar male voice brought a grin to Lexi's face. Focusing on the espresso machine before her, Lexi let the milk froth to just the right thickness. Once happy with its form, she rapped the mug on the counter and flashed a grin at her brother. "Hey yourself! What are you doing here?" A chair scraping across the food court tiles told Lexi her brother was taking a seat, as she finalized her customer's order and accepted payment.

"I'm not sure. Why does one come to a coffee shop, Lex?"

Lexi rolled her eyes at his sarcasm as she processed the payment. Then she wiped down the counter and flipped the tea cloth over her shoulder before turning her attention to him. For four years the Ocean View café had been her part-time job while Lexi studied Bachelor of Youth Work. And not once had Shaun visited during the working week. Curiosity aroused, she rested a hip against the counter. "Ok, what's up?"

"I'd like to order. Is this how you treat all your customers?"

Lexi raised an eyebrow. "Shaun. What are you doing here?" He remained cool, and she held his gaze until he tossed a napkin at her - which she snatched and binned. "Shaun!" Her brother sat back and grinned before looking past her. Then he winked. With a quick head check behind her, Lexi saw her work colleague blushing. "Stop it!" she said, slapping at her brother's arm. "You're such a tease."

A comical ring tone pierced the air, and the playful grin on Shaun's face morphed into an intense study of the countertop. By the topic of conversation, Lexi guessed it was Shaun's boss on the other end of the line, and she straightened up the counter while eavesdropping. From Shaun's side of the conversation, it sounded as if his work site was nearby. When the phone call wrapped up, Shaun cleared his throat, and Lexi turned back to him.

He was rising from his seat and pulling on a Hi-Vis vest, the vibrant sunset orange tone highlighting his tanned skin. "Need to run, sis. I'll be back at lunch for that coffee I never got."

"Is your firm the one working on the new high rise going up next door?" Lexi said, ignoring his sarcastic comment.

He nodded, shouldering his work pack. "That's us. I've got to interview a bloke shortly to oversee the apprentices we've taken on; now listen." The sudden shift in Shaun's tone made her grin. Gone was her flirtatious, playful older brother, and before her, was the serious, overprotective version that bespoke of maturity more advanced than his twenty-five years. Only four years separated them, but sometimes Lexi felt it was more. "There's going to be a lot of fellas floating around here at smoko and lunchtime. Now, I mean it when I say, don't get any ideas. Keep an eye on those younger girls you work with also."

A curt laugh rang out at his comment, and Lexi covered her mouth as she heard it echo around the food court. "Says you?

Who openly flirts with them when they visit me at home?" she said, regaining her composure.

Shaun dismissed his sister's observation. "They know me, and they know it's in fun. I don't know these new fella's I'm working with. So, until I've worked them out, call me protective, or whatever you want, I just want you to watch it around them."

Lexi leaned across the counter as Shaun put his sunglasses on and laid a hand on his arm. "You flatter me, bro. But I'm sure the boys could care less about who serves their coffee."

"It's a guy thing. We stir each other up about any known sisters. They know my sister works here and being the good-looking fella that I am, they'll have already decided they'll want to get a look at you. And, I don't want to hear my sister's name bantered about on the work site."

While his assessment of himself brought a smile to Lexi's face, she could tell he was serious and trying to keep it light at the same time. So, she adjusted her manner to show she'd heard and understood what he was saying. Then Lexi gave him a nod. Shaun always had her best interest in mind, and she saw no reason to doubt him now. "See you at lunch, bro. I'll have that coffee ready."

"You better."

She smiled after Shaun as he headed towards the escalators that would take him to the first floor, then out to the work site. Lexi watched until he slipped from her sight. As far as brothers go, Shaun would top the list. Lexi was proud of him. Though he'd never done well at school, Shaun worked hard at his trade after leaving high school midway through year ten. And soon, he found himself thriving. Now Project Manager on the new work site, Shaun had an income she could only hope to achieve when she finished Uni. Not to mention the fact that most of her friends considered him a double for Matthew Daddario, with his dark hair and hazel eyes – yeah, she was proud of him. And Renee was great for him - much to Tiffany's disgust.

A wry grin tugged on the corner of her mouth as she peeked over her shoulder at her work colleague. As if hearing her thoughts, Tiffany looked over at her and smiled. She was a nice girl; however, Tiffany could never turn Shaun's head enough for him to ask her out. At the ping of the counter bell, Lexi crossed the café to serve a small crowd of customers who had appeared. With a quick brush of her fringe to the side, she chased the non-work-related thoughts from her mind and re-focused on her work. Shaun was right. There was a notable amount of tradies standing out from the other customers in their Hi-Vis clothing. While she heard Tiffany excitedly conversing with them, Lexi kept her head down - paying the young male customers no extra attention.

As the last of the rush hour customers left, Lexi moved out into the dining area to begin cleaning up, when a well-presented young man caught her eye. Reclined on a lounge, the fellow was outfitted in stone colored dress pants and a classic white shirt with sleeves rolled back to his elbows. The daily newspaper held the man's attention. His demeanor oozed charm, and Lexi found herself stealing glances at him as she tidied nearby. Considering herself discreet, she took in his cropped black hair, chiseled jaw, and muscular forearms. A fantasy filled her mind with possibilities - if only she dared to introduce herself to him. That is the type of thing that Hope would do in this circumstance. He looked up. Surprised, Lexi fumbled the loaded tray she held. A hollow tapping sound beside her drew her attention to an empty cup rolling past. She stooped to pick it up, aware of the color licking up her neck and pooling in her cheeks. Embarrassed, she carried the laden tray back to the café, inwardly scolding herself. Unable to stop the impulse, Lexi risked another glance in his direction. He was still watching her. A lopsided grin formed on his face as he turned his attention back to the newspaper.

Safe in her work station, Lexi struggled to remove the young man from her thoughts. His gaze had felt almost physical, and she shivered, remembering the first time his eyes locked on hers. To distract herself, Lexi checked the time and instantly felt a new buzz of excitement tickle her nerves. In under an hour, she would be lounging on the pristine sands of The Valley's main beach. Her beach bag was ready to go, and she could almost taste the ocean salt spray and feel the afternoon sun. Resolved to work just one more hour, Lexi set her mind to working down the clock. And not on a certain dark-eyed man.

THREE

The sand squeaked underfoot as Lexi made her way down the beach toward where Hope had set up a picnic dinner. Shading her eyes against the late afternoon sun, she scanned the surf for the boys. With the warm summer evenings numbered as autumn drew near, they would be taking every chance available to get out on their boards. Lexi stopped to watch the waves, hypnotic as they rolled and crashed against the shore - enjoying the peace that filled her soul every time she visited the beach. It was so beautiful. All of a sudden, distracted by three figures catching a wave a fair way out, she squinted against the late afternoon sun.

"Ten bucks says Nick will get dumped."

Startled at hearing Hope's voice so close, she turned to find herself almost upon the picnic rug Hope had arranged. Lexi kicked her sandals off and knelt onto the rug. Grinning she asked, "Would you have stopped me if I'd just kept walking?"

Hope laughed. "Hmm, maybe. I saw you walking along lost in your own thoughts, and was wondering if you'd seen me here or not."

The array of cut fruit, prepared salads, bread rolls, and drinks laid out over the rug caught Lexi's attention, and her stomach growled - reminding her it was dinner time. "This looks amazing. When did you get time to prepare all this?"

Hope laughed, popping a grape in her mouth. "It's called take away, Hun."

Lexi looked over the spread and selected an apple. She should have known. One of Hope's pet peeves was cooking, and, where possible, she always had someone else do it for her. As the temperature continued to hover in the high 30's, Lexi felt the lure of the water like a whisper in her ear, and she cracked open a bottle of water. In the distance, they watched as the boys caught a wave that would bring them into shore.

"So, how's your brother doing?"

Though Hope's question sounded casual, Lexi grinned as she tossed her hair back. She knew what was behind the question. "He's good. Still with Renee." As she looked out over the water, Hope pretended to be uninterested in Lexi's older brother, while Lexi reminisced over the many times her friend had managed to turn Shaun's head. Shaun liked blondes. So, when Hope had cut her hair into the sassy, choppy style she currently wore, Lexi was sure her friend would steal Shaun's heart. Surprising them both, Shaun had instead asked out raven-headed Renee.

Lexi sighed happily, closing her eyes against the heat of the sun, watching her eyelids turn shades of amber and red. A warmth spread through her body as her mind linked Shaun with the attractive stranger at the café earlier. "You know, speaking of Shaun," Lexi said. "He gave me the riot act earlier. I'm not supposed to entertain any attention from the boys he's working with on the new work site if they visit the café." The girls faced each other and Lexi continued, "But he didn't say anything about fella's he *didn't* work with."

Hope rolled onto her side, propping her head up on her palm. "Tell me."

Mimicking Hope's posture, Lexi filled Hope in on the young man that had caught her eye at work. She wished she'd had the guts to speak with him. As she explained the moment and described his appearance, Lexi's breath caught, and she reached quickly for her water. Hope laughed, and Lexi eyed her over the drink.

"If I heard you right," Hope said. "We are talking about a total interaction time – if you could even call it that – of less than a few seconds. Don't you think you're making a little too much out of it?"

"Maybe," Lexi said, rolling back onto her elbows. "It was a good few seconds though." Something hit her lightly on the side of the head, and she brushed a hand quickly over her hair and face fearing a sand fly. Instead, a grape tumbled down Lexi's chest and into the mat. Glowering at Hope, Lexi picked it up and tossed it back at her. Hope batted it away, raising her eyebrows in return.

"Talk to me when you have a little more than a few seconds of a 'look' to report."

"Well I'm going for a swim," Lexi said, tightening her halter neck bikini top before pulling on a rashie. "You know it's probably a good thing if I don't see him again. I mean, if he could do this to me with just a look, imagine if we were together?" Hope lunged towards her in an effort to shove her off the picnic rug, but Lexi rolled out of her way. "I'm just saying!" she said as she jumped to her feet.

"Get in the water and cool off!" Hope said as she began to rise from the picnic rug.

Challenge extended, Lexi began running down the sand toward the water. Though Hope was a sprinter, Lexi willed her long legs to move quickly through the deep sand, despite the burning that was licking up her legs from the strain. The shallows were in range; she could taste the victory. As Lexi sloshed into the water, she heard Hope closing in behind. Raising her arms, Lexi turned triumphantly. Moments later, Lexi burst through the surface dragging air back into her lungs. Violent coughs racked her frame as she pushed the hair from her eyes and tried to regain her footing against the undertow. "You had to tackle me anyway, didn't you?" Lexi fell silent as Hope's gloating grin suddenly turned playful. Struggling against the undertow, Hope turned away and made for the shore. With a half-interested glance, Lexi looked over her shoulder to see what Hope had been looking at and her eyes went wide.

"STACKS ON!"

With renewed effort, Lexi regained her footing and made for the shore. She could hear the boys behind her. Their laughter and smack of their surfboards on the water nearby told her she didn't stand a chance. They were closing in fast. Unable to help the laughter bubbling out of her as she ran, she caught sight of Trent bringing down Hope, and she forced herself on, laughing harder. Seaweed suddenly smacked her on the side of the head, and she stumbled, peeling it off as Nick's cheering sounded nearby. Lexi's legs felt like lead. They protested each movement, and her lungs burned with exertion though Lexi urged herself on. Just a few more strides and she'd be past the undertow and back on the sand. Where was Dylan? As soon as her intuition warned he was behind her, her legs gave out, and she toppled into the water. A weight fell over her as the undertow dragged her out and she knew it was him. She found her footing once more, and after clawing the hair from her eyes, she smirked at Dylan sprawled in the water before her. "Well that backfired on you, didn't it?" she said, balancing herself against the pull of the tide as he looked up at her; the roll of the waves rocking him beneath her. She held a hand out to him. "Truce?"

Dylan reached up and took the hand she offered. As his cobalt eyes locked on hers, Lexi read the look behind them and tried to tug her hand free moments before he pulled her back into the water. Like a cat, she flipped herself over and glared up at Dylan before batting his hand away, watching as his mouth hitched into a lopsided grin, "C'mon Lex. Truce?"

"Let's go you guys, Nick's eating all the food!"

At Hope's shout from the picnic mat, Lexi squashed her vengeful thoughts. She squinted up at Dylan through her disheveled hair as she placed her hand in his, allowing him to help her up. "Ok. Truce. For now."

Hope waved a hand over what was left of the dinner spread as they approached. Lowering herself onto the rug, Lexi picked up her water bottle again. "Couldn't wait for us, Nick?" He raised a shoulder indifferently at her question and continued to wolf down the contents of his plate. "Ok, so who's thought about our first meeting tomorrow night?" Hope asked. "Do we have to come up with the ideas for youth nights or does Dave organize it all?"

"I think it will go both ways," Trent said, rubbing his chest down with a beach towel before shaking the water from his dreadlocks. "Don't know about you guys but I'm looking forward to the challenge."

As her friends discussed the upcoming Leadership Team meeting, Lexi picked over the remaining salads and fruit trying to ignore the fluttering in her stomach. She still felt unsure about what the Leadership Team would require of her, and she prayed her role would be a minor part.

FOUR

"Hi, Lexi. You're a little early. Dave's in the library."

"Thanks, Linda," Lexi said, with a smile as she stepped past Dave's wife. "Will you be joining us?" The door clicked shut behind her, and Lexi heard the smile in the older lady's voice when she spoke.

"Not for this one. Dave's quite excited about the new format - told me about his ideas over dinner." A crash, followed by a cry, broke off their conversation, and Linda turned to look down the long corridor. "Sorry, Lexi. I put the two monkeys to bed, but sounds like they're up again." She gestured toward the library, and Lexi followed the instruction while watching Linda race toward the clamoring sound of childish voices.

The door gave way at Lexi's light knock, and Dave rose to welcome her. "Lexi, great to see you. Have a seat. The others aren't far off."

"Sorry if I'm a little early."

"No, it's fine. I actually wanted to have a quick chat with you before the others arrive."

Lexi forced a casual smile as she lowered herself into one of the leather tub chairs opposite Dave's desk. Clearing her throat, she asked, "Oh? What about?"

"You seemed reluctant to be a part of this when I mentioned it last Friday. Am I right?"

Lexi blinked. Surprised by the accuracy and bluntness of his comment, she began to feel enclosed in the small room. Dave nodded once as the silence lengthened, returning his attention to the page in front of him. Shifting forward in the seat as excuses and explanations formed in her mind, Lexi found they caught on her tongue. The silence grew until the door behind them flew open, and Nick and Hope walked in mid-conversation. Disappointed that she could not find the words to explain her anxieties, she slumped back in the chair and smiled over her shoulder at her friends entering the room.

"Dylan and Trent are on their way," Nick said as he settled into the matching tub chair next to Lexi's. "Gym session went a bit longer than they thought."

Dave checked his watch. "Ok, well let's get started."

Not wanting to voice her concerns in front of her friends, Lexi pulled out the notebook she'd brought along and penned notes as Dave spoke. Her questions would have to wait. Two pages later, the door opened again as Dylan and Trent entered.

"Great to see you boys could finally make it." Dave's droll tone elicited soft chuckles around the room as the two boys uttered apologies, taking a seat on an old church pew positioned against the side wall. "You two can catch up as we go along," Dave said as he stood and made his way around the room handing each of them a slip of paper. "Friday night we're going to play a revised version of 'Rescuing the Treasure.' It'll be played at night and by flashlight. It's a well-known fact that in difficult times we are refined and our strengths highlighted. So, let's learn a little more about our youth by raising the difficulty level of the game. Ok, I need two teams and a referee, what's it going to be? Show me how you guys will think on your feet."

Having never seen the business side of Dave before, Lexi was unsure if he was teasing them or actually challenging them. She glanced around to her friends and saw the same thoughts mirrored in their expressions.

Then Hope's hand shot into the air. "I say, Lexi and I against Nick and Dylan. Trent can be Ref." Dave nodded. "Done."

"Whoa. Why am I Ref?" Trent asked sitting forward on the pew.

"Because you're good at it."

Grinning at Hope's dismissing answer, Lexi watched Trent as he shared a confused look with Dylan - who snook his head slightly and shrugged before turning his attention back to Dave. Doing likewise, Lexi accepted the folded piece of paper Dave was holding out to her, then he handed Nick a folded piece of paper.

"These are your teams. I have assigned the teams and the captains. You'll also find a map to your safe house. At the bonfire on Friday night, Nick will be handing your team these." Pausing a moment, Dave handed Nick a bag of blue wristbands with one white band visible. "Your Captain wears the white band as well as a blue band." Looking over at her, Dave handed Lexi a bag of red wristbands – a white one also visible inside. "Lexi? Same deal. Midway through the evening, I will blow an air horn, and that signifies the beginning of the game. When you hear the siren, lead your team to the safe house. Once there, your role is to announce the team's captain, give them the white wrist band, and explain the revised game. There will be a box of tools that will help with gameplay, and it is the Captain's job to divvy these out. As you know, the first to rescue the treasure wins. Once your team brings the treasure back to the safe house, pick up your flag and lead them back to the bonfire."

Eyebrows raised as she took a deep breath, Lexi looked up from her notebook filled with notes. "Is this the prep you used to do with Mark and Carla before a Friday night program?"

"Yes."

"Ok, cool. Just wondering," Lexi said, returning her attention back to her notepad. The gloomy sensation of being in over her head crept into Lexi's thoughts once again. A throat clearing brought her attention to Dylan, who was sitting forward on the pew, hands clasped in front of him.

"So, two of us play the game with our assigned team, the Ref's role is obvious, but what do the rest of us do back at the bonfire?"

Dave leaned back in his chair. "Good question. Anyone want to venture a guess?" A moment of silence passed before Dave grinned and linked his fingers behind his head. "Any guesses at all? All of you have been a part of the youth group for several years now. What happens in the later parts of the evening?"

Relief coursed through Lexi as she realized a part of the team she could play very well. What she lacked in leadership, Lexi made up for in hospitality. "The café opens, Dave," she said feeling a sense of confidence about what she could bring to the new Leadership Team. Her smile brightened as she closed her notepad.

Clapping his hands once, Dave pointed at her. "Correct. Carla mentioned more than once she felt overwhelmed some nights in the café while Mark took the youth through the end of evening games. So, I've decided there should be two manning the Café when it opens."

As the boy's collective expressions betrayed their dislike of the idea, Lexi laughed and patted Nick on the thigh with jest. "Don't worry boys, I'll have it covered."

"Actually, all facets of youth nights will be on rotation, so you'll all have a turn in the café."

Laughter dying in her throat at Dave's mention of 'rotation,' Lexi swallowed hard. "So, I'll leave it up to you all to sort out who is going to be in the café Friday night. Then we'll play it week by week and see how we go. Any questions?"

There it was. The part of the Leadership Team Lexi wasn't looking forward to. Dave had asked if they had any questions, she had questions alright but voicing them seemed to be the problem. One thing Lexi knew: she had to find her voice before Friday night.

* * * *

"Ok, so who's first for Café duty?"

Lexi speared at the ice cubes bobbing in her tall glass and waited to see who might answer Trent's question. The meeting had concluded quickly at Dave's due to a phone call. As they left, Nick suggested they continue on at The Valley's Beach-Side Hotel. Sitting under the fairy lights in the alfresco area, Lexi turned her face to the gentle sea breeze and breathed deeply. It was either her or Hope on their team, and she wasn't confident with the alternative. "Well, I'm happy to do it for our team. Who's it going to be out of you boys?"

Dylan and Nick eyed each other over the table. It was clear neither wanted the gig. Nick broke first after the extended silence. "Pretty sure Dylan'd be great at it - I mean, with all that practice getting the morning tea for the boys at the garage." Dylan leaned back in his chair and crossed his arms, an eyebrow hitched up.

Trent held a hand up. "As the Ref for the evening, I'm calling it. Dylan, you're up first, and Nick you can look after the team while they play. Like Dave said duties are on a rotation so . . ."

"Sorry for interrupting, Trent," Nick said. "But, speaking of 'rotation,' you went awfully quiet at that point in the meeting. What's the go?"

"Me?" Lexi said, stalling. She knew the question was aimed at her, though the answer was beyond her grasp.

"Actually, I noticed that too, Nick," Hope said. "Now that I think about it, you went quiet last Friday in Dave's office too. Everything ok?"

Unprepared for their questions, Lexi reached for her drink - painfully aware of the color spilling into her face. "It's nothing new. You all know that I don't like being the center of attention, and I get nervous when speaking in front of people. I mean, a few people, and I'm ok. But the youth group has grown to well over fifty young people. I agreed to be in the Leadership Team thinking I could help plan lessons, set up, or even work the café at the end of the night. But Dave talking about rotations tonight has thrown me." She sipped her drink, then put her glass down and looked at her friends. The waiter reappeared, and Dylan waved him away. "What if I get tongue-tied, or make a fool out of myself? Or worse, pass out? I have passed out before you know. What if I let the team down? I just feel there are stronger people in our group who could step up and fill the role much better than me." Looking at Hope when she felt her friend's hand upon her arm, she encountered a warm gaze shining back at her.

"Sweetie, you're not going to let anybody down. We'll all be working together and . . ."

"Dave said the duties will be on rotation," Lexi said, interrupting Hope. "So, it's fair to say at some stage I'll be required to lead a study group, or run a game, or speak on the stage, or . . ." Trailing off Lexi shook her head. Just explaining things that caused her so much anxiety made her feel silly. Until recently she'd never had to challenge her fear. Besides, she'd never found a reason to. She was happy serving God in the background as an encourager of others, and her Bachelor of Youth Work would end her up in a local government position, or as a one on one counselor, so she'd dodge the spotlight. Taking a deep breath, she ran a hand over her hair. Lexi decided to talk to Dave Friday night about the Leadership Team and suggest he find someone else for the role.

FIVE

"Alright those counters are spotless, go home," Lexi said.

Tiffany was fussy - a trait that most employers desire. But when that fussiness accrued over time, it began to get irritating. Lexi looked at her watch. It was quarter past five on Friday evening, and Tiffany's finish time was five. If Lexi didn't get her out of here soon, the boss would have words with Lexi about her staff management abilities again.

"Ok, ok. I just wanted to make sure all was ready for Michelle in the morning." Tiffany said, turning to face the products on the shelves behind the counter.

Without a second thought, Lexi went to the cupboard where staff stored their belongings, took out Tiffany's designer handbag, and crossed the small workspace to her colleague. "Go home," Lexi said, holding out the handbag. "See you Monday, Tiff. Have a great weekend."

Tiffany took her bag with a resigned grin and headed out of the café. Waving her off before she disappeared down the escalators, Lexi turned and began reconciling the cash register, eager to get home herself. Youth group started at 7:00 p.m., though she was required to be at the bonfire by 6:30 p.m. for set up. And, that wasn't accounting for the time she needed for her chat with Dave.

"You're working late tonight."

The male voice breaking the quiet of the food court startled Lexi, and she spun around, bumping the drawer of the cash register in her haste. The sharp rattle of the coins in their tray echoed loudly around the open space, and her breath rushed out at seeing who was settling himself at the counter. She shook her head slightly as she regained her thoughts and indicated to the cash register. "I . . . I'll be with you in just a m . . . moment." The desire for this guy's return visit had been replaced in her mind with worry about the evening starting in just over an hour. For him to reappear on the cusp of that evening, left Lexi feeling unprepared. With shaking fingers, she finished counting the last of the coins when she heard him clearing his throat behind her.

"Sorry, ma'am. Is it too late to get a drink?"

She turned to face him. His voice was rich, almost cultured, and she grinned. "Oh, no. I mean, we are closed, but it wouldn't take long to warm the machines up for you. What would you like?"

Her question was met with a lingering pause as he seemed to catch himself. He dropped his head as he ran a hand over his dark hair, then he looked at her again, and grinned lopsidedly. "Cappuccino. Please."

"Cappuccino it is. I'll be right back." Once behind the center console on which the cappuccino machine was sitting, Lexi let her breath out. She knew he knew she was nervous. And he was clearly enjoying it! Not to mention, she was sure he also knew she was attracted to him. Shaking her hands to try and rid the tremor in them, Lexi set the beans to grinding while frothing the milk. Once the milk was finished, she expertly added the finishing touches. Taking one more calming breath, Lexi stepped around the console and crossed the café towards him. Her hands were still shaky as she lowered the mug to him, causing it to rattle on the saucer. "There you go. Enjoy." Annoyed at herself for sounding breathless, Lexi turned away to hide the blush she knew was coloring her cheeks. He was one of those impossibly good-looking people you just wonder at, and can't help but be attracted to. But he made her nervous, and a part of her wanted him to leave. All of a sudden, remembering the time, she checked her watch, and her stomach tightened. She had to get going!

"So, what are you up to tonight once you finish up here?"

Not expecting him to make conversation, Lexi glanced over her shoulder and found him regarding her over the rim of his mug. He wasn't in any hurry by the way he appeared. She was about to tell him about the youth group when the words seem to catch over her tongue. She knew the look most gave her when she talked about programs at her church, and realized that she didn't want him looking at her in polite interest with that strained manner. "Oh? Ah, not a great deal. What about you?"

He raised an eyebrow as he sipped his drink. "Avoiding the question?" His gravelly voice was teasing, and she felt goosebumps rise over her arms and tickle her neck. If she withheld that she was going to youth group then she would be lying, but if she did tell him, would he stereotype her and never come back? His phone began ringing, filling the empty Shopping Centre suddenly with music - an 80's rock song she knew well. Lexi relaxed slightly at the reprieve and the thought they shared similar taste in music. He threw the rest of his drink down, then answered the phone The conversation was short and direct while he extracted exact change for his drink, and placed it neatly beside the empty mug. Then, rising from the stool, he shot her a wink and left. Once he was out of sight, Lexi slumped against the counter and dropped her head into her hands. A couple of deep breaths later she tossed her hair back, considered what just happened, then took another glance at her watch: 5:50 p.m. Eyes widening, she quickly put the money in the till and cleaned up the cup and saucer. Running to the staff cupboard, Lexi grabbed her items, ripped off her apron, and ran out of the café, locking it behind her.

* * * *

Fifteen minutes later, Lexi pulled into the driveway, and killing the engine, jumped from her Jeep and ran to the house. She had her hand on the door handle when it opened from the inside, causing her to stumble over the threshold.

Her brother's chuckle greeted her. "I'm used to women falling at my feet, but I never thought one of them would be you."

Grabbing the door frame, Lexi pulled herself back to her feet and pulled a face at Shaun before propelling herself towards the stairs. Halfway up she paused and turned back to him as the door was closing behind him. "Wait. Aren't you coming to youth group?"

A moment later Shaun's head appeared around the door. "Nar. Sorry, sis. Gotta go. See you tomorrow."

"You know, just because Mark and Carla are gone doesn't mean you can't come along and help every now and then," Lexi called out as the door began to close. It opened once more before the latch clicked.

Shaun stepped inside and sighed with tired patience. "I'm taking my new recruit out to get to know him a little better before Monday. A couple of the other boys are meeting us as well. You and your friends have it covered. I'm too old for the church's youth program anyway."

A look of displeasure crossed Lexi's features as she watched the door close behind him. She knew he'd outgrown the youth program, but it was always more fun having him there. Moments later, dressed in distressed jeans and a simple white T-shirt, Lexi glanced at the butterfly wall clock in her room. She should have been gone! The pair of pink thongs poking out from under her bed would have to do for shoes. After roughly tying her hair up into a messy bun, Lexi grabbed her favored perfume, and throwing it in her bag, raced back downstairs.

Thankful that Pastor Walker only lived two suburbs away, she found herself pulling into his small Farmlet property within twenty minutes. The long winding driveway was lined with vehicles, and Lexi craned her neck hoping for a spot close to the homestead. With an expression of cheer, Lexi pulled into a spot next to Nick's Black Clubsport and killed the engine. A quick check of her watch told her there wasn't enough time to speak with Dave before the night got started, and she took a moment to compose herself. A few deep breaths and a prayer for confidence later, she pulled out her perfume and spritzed herself with the light oriental scent. Lexi stepped down from her Jeep as prayers for confidence continued in her mind. She passed the vehicles parked alongside the house when one grabbed her attention, and Lexi stopped. The sight of a Harley Davidson Motorbike parked amongst them was odd; however, she stepped closer to the bike, and deeply breathed in the scent of new leather and polished chrome. There was only one person she knew who wanted one of these. "What do you think?"

A smile broke out on her face as the voice behind her proved her suspicions correct. Turning slowly, Lexi watched as Dylan crossed the gravel driveway towards her. Hands deep in the pockets of his jeans, he grinned like a Cheshire cat as he approached. The homestead lanterns illuminated his ruffled blond hair and eyes as they lingered on the bike behind her. Lexi thumbed over her shoulder. "Yours?"

Dylan dipped his head. "You bet."

Lexi felt her jaw drop, and she turned to look at the red trim and silver chrome bike once again. "You couldn't seriously have saved enough money to buy one of these yet!"

"Why not?" Dylan asked quietly. "I've been working since I was sixteen."

She coughed a laugh as she looked up at him. "As an apprentice! I know what apprentices earn."

He chuckled. "A Diesel Mechanic's apprenticeship is only four years, Lex, and I've been qualified for three years now." Lexi dodged his playful jab. "Remember when you lot got your licenses and went out every weekend? Who didn't go with you?" Nodding as memories flashed to mind, she shrugged. "Well, now I wish I'd done the same. Least then I'd own my wheels." Aware once more of the time, Lexi turned and continued her way to the rear of the house.

Dylan fell into step beside her. "So, what were you doing out here anyway?" he asked. "We were expecting you to arrive a good twenty minutes ago."

"Oh, I was running late from work and needed a moment to pray for confidence before the evening started. What were *you* doing out here?" Lexi turned an accusing gaze on Dylan as they rounded the homestead. His smile was bright and betrayed him. She poked a finger in his arm. "You were checking on the bike, weren't you?"

Their names were called, and Lexi turned her attention from Dylan and searched the bonfire for who was calling them. A smile grew on her face as she watched the young people gather around the fire, filling the air with chatter and laughter. Music was playing while the food was being dished out. Lexi's smile faded as she remembered her duties for the evening.

"Lexi, Dylan, over here." Dave stood at the rear door of Pastor Walker's home, waving them over.

After acknowledging she'd seen him, Lexi ignored the unwanted negative thoughts buzzing in her mind and made her way over to Dave. Once inside, she found Trent, Hope, and Nick seated just inside the house on the kitchen bench. "Hi all, sorry I was late. Got held up at work."

"Don't worry about it; we haven't quite started," Dave said, dismissing her apology with a wave of his hand as he ushered them inside.

Stomach rolling with nerves, Lexi crossed her legs and tried to appear as relaxed and as excited as her friends.

Standing before them, Dave clapped his hands. Radiating enthusiasm, he called the group to order. "Ok guys. It's not a big night ahead. Pastor Walker has it mostly covered. We are just looking after the game component for the evening. We have a moment before he's going to call you all out and introduce you as our new youth group leaders."

Dave's voice faded away as Lexi's mind stuck on the last thing he said – call you out . . . introduce you . . . youth group leaders! She swallowed hard as a cool sweat made itself known on her palms. Reaching up, she undid her hair, shook it out, and retied it. Mind distracted, she caught the end of Dave's pep talk.

" . . . so, what did you all decide on for Café duty? Who's up first?" "Lexi from our team and I think Dylan from the boys," Hope said.

All of a sudden, a shrill whistle rang out from the bonfire, and they craned their necks to look outside. Dave stood and crossed the room to open the door. "Looks like we're up. Let's go."

One by one the boys followed Dave as Lexi willed her legs to move. She could see forty plus young people had turned out. And they were eager to see who appeared from the house, no doubt trying to figure out who had been chosen as the new leaders.

Firm fingers encased Lexi's upper arm, lifting her from the stool. "Come on, sweetie, you'll be fine."

Once out of the house with Hope, Lexi kept her eyes trained on Pastor Walker. When they were all standing together at the front of the gathering, Lexi moistened her lips, feeling uncomfortably hot in front of the fire. She listened as they were introduced. One by one her friends were introduced to cheers and applause, though, when her name was called, the din rose notably.

A slight grin flickered on her face as she glanced at the friends beside her and found the same curious expressions mirrored back at her. Why were the youth so excited and eagerly waving at her?

"See you have a few fans out there," Hope said, leaning towards her. "This won't be so bad after all."

Lexi sniffed, surprise marking her words as she looked over the gathered young people before them. "No, perhaps not."

SIX

The frying pan popped and sizzled beside her, and scraping a spoon up the edge of the pan, Lexi sampled the new variation of scrambled eggs she was cooking. Perfect. A soft ping echoed over the open plan living area as the toast popped up. Sashaying across the room, Lexi finished setting the table for breakfast just as the floor above her creaked. The family was stirring. On her way back to the kitchen to gather the meal, she passed Shaun shuffling towards the table. Eyes barely open, he acknowledged her sleepily. "Good morning!" she said, her tone bright and cheerful.

"Why do you always have to be so cheery in the morning?"

With a grin over her shoulder at his protest, Lexi continued to the kitchen to dish up the eggs and collect the toast. After returning to the table, Lexi chose a seat opposite her brother and smiled at him. "What have you got planned for the day, Bro?"

Shaun ran a hand down his face and blinked slowly before reaching for the eggs. "Going to a soccer match with some boys from work. The new recruit we took out Friday night loves soccer and thinks we all need an education." He yawned as he tilted his phone towards him. "Matter of fact, Brad will be here any minute."

"Cool. Sounds like fun," Lexi said, taking a piece of toast and buttering it as her parents joined them at the table.

A half an hour later, the breakfast table was strewn with crumbs and dirty dishes when the doorbell interrupted the conversation. Taking the opportunity, Lexi collected the plates as Shaun went to answer the door.

"Let me do those; you made breakfast." At her mum's voice, Lexi turned to protest. But her mum silenced her with a look. "Those assignments won't do themselves, and you said they had to be done by Monday. Go."

Making a face at her mum, Lexi turned to leave the kitchen just as Shaun reentered - followed by a man she figured was Brad. The fellow was a little shorter than her brother's 6 foot 1 inch, but he was broader across the shoulders. And he filled out his casual shirt very well. Curious, Lexi stalled at the fridge, pretending to be looking for a drink. Casually eavesdropping on the conversation they were having with her father at the dining table, Lexi thought the visitor's voice sounded familiar as he complimented the house and décor. There was something familiar about how he finished his words.

"Lexi. Room!"

Jumping at her mum's growl, she forgot about the guest, grabbed an iced tea, and shut the fridge door. "Going!"

"Oh, that's my sister Lexi."

She froze hearing her brother's voice behind her. Heat spilled into Lexi's face as she remembered the young man in their midst. There was no escaping the embarrassment of being scolded in front of him, so Lexi tossed her hair back as she turned to greet the guest with her most welcoming smile. Her voice caught in her throat. The man from the café! At their dining table ! Her pause must have been longer than thought, as Shaun spoke before she could. "Have you two already met?" Thankful for the drink in her hands, Lexi cracked it open and took a few mouthfuls before venturing to speak.

The young man rose and answered Shaun's question as he crossed the floor towards her. "We have, although not formally." He stopped before Lexi and smiled. A knowing smile she read instantly, though Lexi smiled back at him as she recapped her drink. He offered his hand. "I'm Brad."

She took the hand he offered and tipped her head in greeting, "Lexi."

Brad's touch lingered longer than necessary, giving time for his appealing scent of spices and musk to envelope her - blocking out the room until only his presence remained. "Ok, so we'll be going now."

Blinking, Lexi brought Shaun into focus, standing beside Brad. Shaun's expression was clear as he looked at her sternly, his mouth pressed into a thin line. Her brother's intimidating gaze sent a clear message: "No!"

Lexi took the hint and withdrew her hand from Brad's. Tipping her drink at the boys, she wished them a good day on a catch of breath. Then she left the room before anything more could be said. Once her bedroom door had closed behind her, Lexi leaned back against it and sighed. Great, the young man who'd monopolized her thoughts since she first saw him, worked for her brother. And judging by the look in Shaun's eyes, Brad was one of the boys his warning applied to. She sipped her drink and looked around her room for a distraction. Her desk sat under the window, the morning light spilled over it highlighting the mass of paperwork she had to get through before Monday. Distraction found, she pushed off the door and moved to her desk.

*   *   *   *

Lexi checked her watch. Ten minutes of class remaining before she could go home. Patience wearing thin, she packed her books up, pushed them to the edge of her desk, and tried to focus on the lecturer. She normally enjoyed the class, 'Working with Young People with Complex Issues,' but Lexi was itching to get away and clear her thoughts. To learn that Brad was off limits made her heart heavy. And, certainly not needed on top of the unexpected enthusiasm from the young people at church. Why were they so excited? What had she done that made her so popular? As she tried to work out the two issues, Lexi rested her chin in her palm and tuned out the lecturer who was now waving a piece of paper. " . . . forty percent of your final grade . . ."

Lexi looked up. The feeling of missing something important crashed over her.

"Get to it. Class dismissed."

The mass exodus from the classroom commenced, and Lexi found herself stranded in her seat until the passages on either side of her had cleared. The stampeding subsided as fast as it started, and Lexi collected her books while wondering if she should ask the teacher or a fellow student what she'd missed. A fellow student would be less scary she decided, as she headed down the lecture theatre steps, only to find her path blocked by the lecturer himself.

"Lexi, could the worried expression you wear have anything to do with you tuning me out in the last ten minutes of class?" her professor asked.

Whoa. Lexi frowned. Honesty was the only option, not that she would lie, but somehow, he already knew the reason for her concern. She sighed, "I'm sorry, sir. I just have a lot on my mind at the moment. What did I miss?"

His glassy teal eyes took on a smile, though his face remained stony. The professor returned to his lectern and pulled out a piece of paper. The man held it out, though he didn't look at her again. Without a word, Lexi hurriedly took the piece of paper and left the lecture theatre. The moment the heavy doors closed behind her, she blew her breath out and read the piece of paper. Mere steps from the double doors leading outside, Lexi halted. Her heart slammed double time as Lexi re-read: *Major Assessment-Plan and conduct youth event. Perform presentation on the activity in class. This assessment accounts for forty percent of your final grade.*

Planning, she could do. In fact, it was a passion. Conducting events? Not so much! Lexi preferred being part of the support crew, so that part of the assignment, in itself, was a test. Presentations were a no go. Just the idea caused her heart to race and blood recede. Her tongue suddenly feeling far too big for her mouth, Lexi reached for her water. After a few mouthfuls, Lexi closed the container and slowly continued toward the car, mind whirling. "This is not happening," she muttered as she opened the car door and dumped her bags on the passenger side seat. Public presentations were unmentioned in the course syllabus - she'd checked before enrolling. No, the course she'd chosen was one that enabled her to do what she wanted to do, while avoiding what she didn't want to do. And now, in an ironic twist, she had to face her fear or risk four years of study. Lexi growled as she started the engine, pulled out of the car park, and headed for home - praying for confidence.

SEVEN

The familiar thud and crash of pins scattering in their lanes greeted Lexi, as she stepped into the foyer of the city's Ten Pin bowling center. Monthly socials with church friends were always a lot of fun, but she particularly loved the bowling nights. After paying for her games and a quick chat with the receptionist, Lexi headed to the rack to pick out her bowling ball. Nick approached and paused alongside her as he squinted at her suspiciously. The disco lights above them reflected in Nick's grey eyes, and Lexi stared back at him. "What's up, Nick?"

"Oh, nothing. I just have a feeling it's going to be a great night."

Nick's manner made a tingle of anticipation zip up Lexi's spine. He knew something she didn't, and by the teasing glint in his eyes, he wasn't about to give away any hints. She wouldn't beg – as she guessed that's what he wanted. Instead, she'd keep her dignity in place and play it cool. After selecting a ball, Lexi grinned as she stepped around Nick and headed for the lanes.

Aware of his trailing presence, Lexi acted oblivious while scanning for what might have him so smug.

"Welcome guys!" Dave said as he came alongside Lexi and Nick.

"Hi, Dave," Lexi said distractedly while continuing to scan the room. Nothing seemed out of the ordinary: Hope was animatedly talking to two men sitting opposite her; Dylan was about to bowl; teenagers were dancing to the pumping music; and, Trent was at the snack bar.

"There is a great turn out tonight. We even have a newbie with us – he's a little older, but we'll welcome him all the same," Dave continued. And Lexi smiled acknowledging his comment. "Perhaps if he enjoys tonight, he might come along to our adult programs. Anyway, we can sort that out later. You guys aren't on duty, as such, but you still have a responsibility toward the young people. Keep an eye on them, ok? Have fun."

As Dave speared off from them, Lexi saw he joined a game in progress, and she glanced at Nick once more. "What lane were you playing at?

Before Nick answered her, Lexi noticed Hope stand up and make her way over to them, while the two men she was speaking with turned around.

"Be good," Nick teased

Lexi's head snapped around at Nick's comment, but he jogged lazily toward Trent. Lexi's eyes narrowed as she watched Nick disappear. What was he up too?

"Hey!" Hope's voice broke into Lexi's thoughts, startling her. "Why is Shaun bringing a workmate to youth group instead of his girlfriend?"

The other girl's hopeful expression erased Nick from Lexi's thoughts, and she flicked a glance past Hope to see who Shaun was with.

"Not that I'm complaining or anything," Hope continued. "It's been months since I saw him at a monthly social, and his friend is super-hot."

"I have no idea," Lexi muttered, more to her own inner question than Hope's query as she spotted Brad sitting along-side Shaun. Thrusting her bag at Hope, Lexi darted away, saying "I'll be back with drinks." Signaling the waitress over, Lexi laid a hand over her stomach as it cramped with excitement. The Alley Café was usually teeming with customers, but it was a slow night. Rattled, Lexi took a deep breath to settle her nerves.

"Hi, what will it be?" the waitress asked.

"Two beers, thanks."

Open mouthed, Lexi turned at the male voice beside her and clutched the countertop. Brad aimed his perfect smile at her, and her stomach flipped. "Avoiding me?"

The server returned with the order, and handing the icy beers to Brad, turned to Lexi. "Anything else?"

What did she want? "Um, two lemonades, please." As the waitress scurried off, Lexi cleared her throat. She *was* avoiding him, but she wasn't about to tell him that. "No, not at all. Just surprised to see you here." "Good surprise?"

"No, I mean yeah! It's just that it's youth night . . . and you're a bit . . ."

Brad's gaze locked on Lexi as he waited for her to answer him, the glint in his eyes evident despite the smoky room. "I'm a bit . . . what?"

"Old? I mean, older. You're a bit too old to be at a youth social," Lexi said, changing her weight and tucking her hair behind her ears. She hated how she'd lost the ability to speak. "Um, what are you doing here?" She knew the color of her face would shame a fire hydrant, and Lexi hoped that in the dim light Brad wouldn't notice. Looking for a distraction, Lexi took the straw poking out of one of the glasses of lemonade between her teeth and took a deep gulp of the cold liquid. Brad chuckled, and she felt her insides warm.

"I took your brother out to a soccer game this afternoon, and we spotted the church bus parked out front on our way home.

Shaun mentioned your involvement in the church's monthly socials, so I suggested we pop in to say 'hi.'"

A throat clearing beside her drew Lexi's attention to the waitress waiting for her to pay for the drinks. Uttering an apology, she reached for her wallet and handed over the money. Then she clumsily scooped up her drinks and turned to Brad. "Hi then." As she returned to her lane, she noticed Brad fall into step beside her.

"Shaun and I are playing with you and your friend, Hope. You don't mind, do you?"

"Not at all," Lexi said, shooting him a quick smile. She placed the drinks on the table between the seats, then sat down to put on her bowling shoes. Bowling was the least elegant sport she could play in the presence of attractive company, and Lexi regretted wearing her wide leg jeans and Captain America T-shirt. Pushing the conceited thoughts from her mind, Lexi joined in the friendly banter within her team as well as the friendly mockery between teams. The night was lively and full of laughter, and Lexi happily participated in the obligatory tunnel ball style bowling on frame ten. In the end, their team won the night, thanks to Shaun bowling a personal best of 270.

"Free drinks and pool for us!" Hope said, kicking off her bowling shoes.

Lexi high fived Hope. "Now that's a game I *can* play!"

"And by drinks, she means no beers," Shaun said, slapping Brad on the back. "This is a church event man."

A slight blush crept over Brad's bronzed skin at Shaun's comment, but Lexi noticed he took the reproof graciously. A character trait she added to the positive list growing in her mind.

After all the lanes were packed up, and shoes were returned, Dave led the group to the game zone adjacent to the bowling alley. The pool table sat in a low-lit area of the room, and seeing it unmanned, Lexi hurried her pace. It was rare for the table to be unattended on a night when the zone was full to capacity, and she didn't want to miss her game.

"Rack 'em up, Lex," Dylan called to her as she reached for the pool rack.

With a glance over her shoulder, Lexi saw Hope perch on a bar stool beside Nick, Trent, and Shaun as Dylan and Brad reached for cues.

"How do the teams work?" Brad asked, chalking his cue.

As Lexi leaned over the table to line the rack up, she looked at Dylan. "I say the team that won gets to go first." Without prompting, Shaun crossed the room and plucked the pool cue from Dylan's hands as Lexi removed the rack and hung it back up.

"First round," she said. "Boys against girls!"

The game of pool relaxed Lexi, and she soon found herself unwinding and forgetting about her unflattering outfit. She delighted that the cramping in her stomach had lessened - even though butterflies tumbled inside Lexi each time her eyes connected with Brad's. The attention he was paying her made her feel a little giddy and, she liked it. There was only one problem: Shaun wouldn't. And he had already indicated so. After sinking the final ball with her trademark shot, Lexi handed her cue to Dylan before taking his seat at the table. As the next round started, Lexi watched as Shaun and Brad took on Dylan and Nick, while Trent and Hope went to check on the youth. Shaun may not like the attention Brad was giving her, but it wasn't every day a man like Brad showed interest in her; so, Lexi was going to enjoy it while it lasted.

EIGHT

Legs crossed, chin propped on a palm, and her other arm limp across her lap, Lexi sat in her thinking pose on the back patio. She stared blankly into the yard while watching the midday sun cast ever-changing shadows across their lawn, raking her brain for youth event ideas. None were coming, just random thoughts of what the shadows looked like as they danced across the lawn before her. She needed a cuppa. That would help the thinking process. After stretching her arms above her head, Lexi stood to make her way back into their home when her eyes fell upon her phone. Maybe she could give Dave a call. He always had great ideas. If she could see him today and thrash out some ideas, then she could move past the block in her mind. Plus, there was the other matter that she still needed to discuss with him.

"Lexi, I need to talk to you."

"Just a quick second," she said, holding a hand up to Shaun as he stepped out onto the patio while she dialed Dave's number. As the phone began to ring, she glanced at her brother, and immediately disconnected the call after noting his expression. "What's up? You ok?"

Shaun pulled out the patio chair opposite Lexi with force. After tossing his phone and keys onto the table before him, he sat heavily and looked at her. She raised an eyebrow. Her brother was agitated, and something inside her said she had a part in it. He shook his head. "Look, I'm sure you've figured out that Brad's into you, and I'm hoping you're not considering dating him."

Confused, Lexi leaned forward. "Are you mad at me or something?"

Irritation emanated from him as he looked at her, and she met his challenging expression with one of her own. She hated fighting with her brother, but she wasn't about to take his issues undeservedly.

"No," he said. "I'm not. *Yet.* But I saw the way you two were looking at each other last night - the whole room saw it. I'll tell you this again. I don't want you anywhere near the boys I work with, and if I hear your name thrown around on the work site . . ." he trailed off, but the steel in his eyes finished the sentence.

Silence passed between them for a moment until Lexi's phone rang, splitting the tension with its cheerful melody. She looked at the screen. It was Dave. Lexi silenced it and looked back at Shaun. She did not want to disappoint her brother, but her intuition whispered that was exactly what was going to happen - no matter how she played her cards. Lexi sighed.

Shaun gathered his things and rose, jaw locked in place. "Don't worry about it, sis. Your silence says enough." He stalked off before she could say anything, but she didn't know what to say!

Frustrated, Lexi slapped her palm against her forehead and tried to think through how to deal with the inevitable, when her phone rang again. After checking the phone, she frowned. Why was work calling her on Sunday? "Hello, Lexi speaking."

"Hi Lexi, it's Michelle. Can you cover me today? I'm not well and need to go home." The stuffy sound of Michelle's voice confirmed the girl wasn't well, as did the sneezing that followed her sentence.

"Sure. Give me a half hour to get there."

"Thanks, Lexi."

More sneezing sounded down the line before the phone disconnected, and Lexi grinned. Work would now replace her planned brainstorming afternoon. Her assignment, conversation with Dave, and issues with Shaun would have to wait.

*　*　*　*

Things were quiet at the café when Lexi arrived to cover for Michelle. The girl was indeed sick as she'd described; her natural creamy complexion had turned a shade whiter, and her reddened nose created an amusing contrast. Lexi smiled sympathetically at Michelle as the girl untied her apron and collected her things. "You take a few days off, ok?" Lexi said as she affixed her own apron. "I will," Michelle said, just before sneezing into a tissue. "I'm hoping it's just hay fever. Thanks again for covering for me."

After Michelle disappeared from sight, Lexi checked her watch - 2:00 p.m. Only three hours left of the shift, then she would hit the books and get her ideas down on paper. Once that was done Lexi would ring Dave and discuss her ideas with him. Sunday afternoon was a shift Lexi only worked if a staff member was sick or on holiday. Hands on hips she looked around the quiet shopping center, then around her workplace. All was in place, dishes were done, and condiments replenished. The fridge was stocked, and counters cleaned down. The counter bell chimed and thankful for a customer to serve, Lexi moved around the center console and stopped.

"So, I'm sure you're avoiding me."

Unable to help the smile that spread across her face at seeing Brad sitting at the counter, Lexi crossed her arms. The red sports branded singlet he wore showed off a distracting set of biceps. Raising an eyebrow, Lexi questioned, "Oh? What makes you think that?"

"Well, you disappeared pretty quick after bowling. And I was kind of hoping we could have caught up afterward for a drink or something."

Surprised at his candor, Lexi cleared her throat as she brushed the fringe out of her eyes, "Oh yeah, sorry. just have a lot going on at the moment." Brad held her gaze until she looked away. A strange sensation of vulnerability settled over Lexi as her gaze swept the empty food court, hoping for a customer to appear. A light bang of a door against its hinge brought her attention back to the café, and she turned back to Brad and noticed he was gone. With a small step towards the counter, she scanned the other side of the empty food court for him.

"Now, you're not going to tell me you're too busy for a drink?"

Gasping, Lexi spun around and stepped back into the counter as Brad moved towards her.

"What time do you finish work?"

Her hands gripped the counter behind her as her heart slammed into overdrive. "Ah, c . . . customers aren't m . . . meant to be back here."

Brad smiled and rested an arm on the counter behind her. "What time do you finish work?" His repeated question told her two things: he had no intention of moving until she agreed to have a drink with him, and Shaun was about to be very disappointed in her.

She moistened her lips. "I f . . . finish at 5:00 p.m."

He straightened after a moment, glanced around the food court, then locked gazes with her once more. "Meet me by the pier?" Brad murmured the request as he gently swept his fingers across her forehead, removing the fringe that had fallen into her eyes. The touch left Lexi with few abilities beyond shakily nodding her head. A moment later, as she watched Brad leave the cafe, Lexi relaxed her grip on the counter and shook out her hands. Why did they shake whenever Brad was around?

Excitement and nervousness began to stir inside her, making it difficult to concentrate as the day went on - putting a question mark over her professionalism. It was unlike her to fumble a saucer and spill the contents of the cup resting on it, and she'd never served the wrong slice to a customer before. When she sugared an order that the client requested unsweetened, Lexi found her anxiety mushrooming.

The hours dragged by, and Lexi's stomach was feeling like a tangled ball of wool. She needed to go for a run or a long walk to unwind. Looking at her watch, Lexi knew that wasn't an option. Brad would be waiting for her to show up. Considering the possible fall out of their beach-side catch-up, Lexi impulsively reached for her phone wanting to cancel - Shaun's warning echoing in her ears. She paused; brow crinkled. There must be aspects of Brad's nature that were good. He did come to youth social, and her brother had been out socially with him a couple of times. Curiosity aroused, Lexi put her phone down as a new interest in the evening flashed through her mind. Perhaps they shared more in common than just music?

NINE

Thankful the working day had finished, Lexi stopped at her car to change before meeting up with Brad. With a grateful sigh, she shook her hair loose and teased it up a little. Pulling the beach bag from the boot of her car, Lexi crawled into the backseat and quickly changed into a pair of sandals, a cotton patterned ankle-length skirt, and simple white halter racer-back singlet.

Still unable to believe what she was doing, Lexi locked her car and headed across the street to the concrete steps leading down to the beach. Lexi's nervousness renewed with each slap of her sandals on the hot bitumen. At the top of the stairs that led down to the creamy sand, she looked out over the dunes to where Brad waited. Lexi sucked in a breath and took a moment to pull herself together. Spotting a solo person seated a stone's throw from the pier on a large blanket with a picnic basket beside him, Lexi's heart skipped a beat. There he was. A prayer and short pep-talk-to-self later, she skipped down the steps and headed towards him.

Brad rose as she approached, laying aside the book he was reading – another thing they had in common she noted – and smiled at her.

Lexi took the hand he offered and knelt onto the blanket. Once she was settled, Brad sat opposite Lexi and continued to gaze at her. "Hi," she softly said.

"Hi." Brad squinted at her, assessing. "You nervous?"

Laughter, a little too bright, tumbled out of her and Lexi blushed, falling silent. How stupid it sounded to be nervous! But she was! Her palms were clammy, and her mouth was dry. She dared not speak for fear of sounding breathless. Brad reached for the picnic basket and pulled out a bottle of non-alcoholic wine. Impressed, Lexi watched him pour a glass for her before pouring one for himself.

"Well, I'm nervous. I didn't think you were going to show."

She finished her glass in a few deep gulps, then tried her voice. "Why wouldn't I?"

"Because of Shaun."

She frowned. "Shaun?"

Brad relaxed onto the mat and propped himself up on an elbow while sipping his drink - his gaze forward as he looked out to the water.

Taking the opportunity, Lexi allowed herself an admiring glance over his exposed arms. A tribal tattoo on the underside of his right bicep made her pulse jump, and she looked away as he turned back to her.

"Yeah, we've had words. I know Shaun doesn't want me seeing you. And I know he's spoken to you about keeping your distance."

A sense of gloom settled over her at Brad's words, and she moved uncomfortably on the blanket. "So, why do you want to see me so much?" Lexi said, turning her gaze back to him, only to find him studying her openly. His eyes were soft and almost adoring as they traveled her face. Lexi trembled, once again feeling vulnerable in his company.

A whisper of a smile began to tug at the corner of his mouth, and he dropped his head in a gesture of defeat. "I don't know, Lexi. I guess some people you just need to be around. There's something about you that's grabbed me. And I want to find out what that thing is."

His statement, so unexpected and flattering, shocked her, and Lexi drew a sharp breath as his focus dropped to her mouth. Blood poured into her face, and she tried to think of a response. Brad's open manner had her off guard once again. On top of his undeniable attraction, Lexi felt like she was traveling shaky ground. A feeling of being in over her head dawned on Lexi, and she turned to look back at the car park.

"Sorry if I've made you uncomfortable." Brad's quiet words drew her attention back to him, and Lexi took in his profile as he looked out over the water. The setting sun had turned his tanned skin to a smooth bronze and highlighted his perfect features.

Thoughts careened through Lexi's confused mind as she studied him, the most prominent being: "Why is he interested in me?" She'd had a boyfriend before, and the odd date here and there. But Brad's intense attraction? Her conscious cautioned her. But why?

Brad ruffled his black hair as he turned back to her, and Lexi caught a hint of the blue tones that reflected under the setting sun. "What do you want to do? I don't want you to be uncomfortable with me."

She sighed, "I should go. Maybe we can do this another time?" Brad nodded and began to pack up when Lexi caught sight of the gold lettering on the book beside him. "What is that?" Her question came out blunter than intended, and his surprised expression told her it was his turn to be caught off guard. Brad held the book up. "You mean this?"

Speechless Lexi gazed at the Bible in his hand Her mouth dropped open, and she struggled to form words. But none came forth.

She heard him chuckle and glared at him as he rose to stand before her.

"Lexi, look. I'm really into you. You're different from any other girl I've met, and I know it's because of this."

Her eyes swept the Bible once again as Brad gestured towards it, and she took the chance to ask: "Why did you really come to youth group the other night?"

Brad grinned as he rubbed the back of his neck. "Ok, you got me. I did suggest we drop in to say 'Hi.' But that's the excuse I gave Shaun. What I really wanted was to see you again."

At a loss, Lexi stared at him. Confusion reigned, and she'd never felt so conflicted. When Brad took her hand, the feeling of his strong fingers entwining with hers drove the air from Lexi's lungs. "Come on. I'll walk you back to your car."

As Brad began to lead her down the beach toward the car park, Lexi found herself unsure if she wanted to leave. Everything was perfect - except for her own thoughts, which were a mess.

At her car, Brad released her hand and took a step back. "I'll wait until you're on your way."

As the sun slipped beneath the horizon, taking with it the last of the day's light, Lexi was thankful for the approaching dusk. It hid the frustrated tears pooling in her eyes. With a heavy heart, she unlocked her car and climbed inside. With a last look at Brad, Lexi gave a weak wave and drove off toward home - tears running down her cheeks and prayers for guidance in her mind.

TEN

Turning her pen end for end on her open books, Lexi sat in the lecture theatre waiting for the Professor to arrive. With thoughts of Brad and stressful assignments swirling around in her mind, the last thing she needed was a tardy professor. While most of the theatre had emptied out, the remaining students used the lag time to talk amongst themselves or study. But Lexi couldn't focus. The more she tried to concentrate, the more her mind evaded her.

She yawned widely, paying for a sleepless night, and looked out the window beside her. It was a cloudless day. A bright blue sky draped the rolling mountain range in the distance and the stately gum trees around campus. On a whim, Lexi collected her books, strode down the stairs, and left the theatre without looking back. Sitting was not helping sort through the issues crowding her mind. A Leadership Team meeting was scheduled for that evening; so, Lexi would ensure that she was at Dave's early enough to talk to him.

Once she arrived home, Lexi headed to the kitchen to make herself a cup of tea and a list of points she wanted to discuss with Dave. A note from her mum, stuck to the refrigerator door, greeted Lexi as she reached inside for the milk. She plucked the note from under the magnet and read: *Whoever gets this note first, please make dinner for the family. Your father and I will be home late. S.E.S. meeting after work. Love, Mum.*

Lexi checked the time. It was just after 5:00 p.m. and the Leadership Team meeting started at 7:00 p.m. She wanted to be there by 6:00 p.m. "Things just keep getting in the way," Lexi thought as she took the milk out and elbowed the door shut. Determined to continue to plan, Lexi finished making her cup of tea and picked up the phone to order takeaway. Once it was ordered and paid for, she took a different color pen and scrawled on the bottom of her mum's note: *Hey Bro! Had to go out. Dinner is ordered and paid for – will arrive at 7:30 p.m. Lex. X*

Sticking the note back under the magnet, Lexi threw back the remainder of her tea and raced upstairs to change. By 6:00 p.m. She'd be at Dave's, and all going well from there, she'd be home again by 7:30 p.m. to have dinner with her family - worry-free.

*   *   *   *

Dave's home was opened up, enjoying the warmer than average winter evening, and Lexi was sure she could smell a roast cooking. Uttering a prayer that she would be able to put words to her concerns, Lexi shouldered her bag and stepped out of her car.

The door opened as she approached on the cobbled pathway, and Dave stood silhouetted in the doorway. He greeted her, and she heard the smile in his voice. "I've been expecting you. Come in."

"Really? Why's that?" Lexi asked, stepping past him into the lounge room. Already knowing the answer, she liked testing out Dave's intuitive skills. It interested her how he could read people so well. The door behind her shut, and she flicked a glance at him as she took a seat on the couch, chuckling at his expression. He knew.

Dave took the seat adjacent to her and waited for Lexi to speak. Levity vanished as she readied herself to let him, and her friends, down. She took a deep breath. "I don't think I can do this Leadership Team thing, Dave. I think you need to find someone else to take my place." Not meeting his eyes as she spoke, Lexi was aware of how much she was fidgeting and made an effort to still herself. A quiet moment passed before she heard Dave relax back into his chair and let a breath out. She looked at him.

"I knew you were feeling uncertain, Lexi, but thought you'd right yourself within the team."

Uncertainty filled her at his words, and Lexi was ready to explain when Dave signaled he wasn't finished.

He looked at her as if he was trying to pick his words carefully. "Do you know why the five of you are together as part of the reformatted Youth Group?"

She shook her head.

"Me either. But knowing each of you, I have my suspicions as to why God has brought you all together. Are you willing to trust Him on this?"

"Have faith in other words?" Lexi asked. Running a hand over her hair, she let out a breath and shrugged. "I don't know." Dave scooted forward in his chair and ran a hand down his face - his brow furrowed, reflecting the need to find the right words. "Lexi, have you ever heard the expression, 'God doesn't call the qualified, He qualifies the called.'"

She shook her head again. The room fell silent as Dave left the sentence hang heavily in the air. Unsure of what she was being called *to*, Lexi knew Dave was asking her to exercise her faith.

Exercise her faith AND trust that her part in the Leadership Team was in God's plan for her. She sank back into the sofa. "Ok. Well, you know I get horrible anxiety in front of crowds and when I'm speaking in front of people. I don't want to have a panic attack or faint in front of anyone."

"Lexi, God, is aware of your struggles; so, find comfort. He wouldn't ask you to do anything that you couldn't do."

"That may be, Dave. But in the meantime, could we take things slowly? You know, work me up to, oh, I don't know, say Hope's level of confidence?"

Dave laughed. "Of course. We'll keep your rotations to your comfort levels. But keep praying about how God wants to use you on the team, Lexi."

A glimmer of hope poked through the clouds in her mind, and Lexi began to feel the seemingly hopeless situation start to look like an opportunity. Excitement began to tickle her spirit at the idea that God was calling *her*! "But to what?" she wondered.

"So, what's the other thing bothering you?" Dave asked, sitting back in his seat.

Lexi cleared her throat and glanced at the wall clock. It was near 7:00 p.m. and the others would be arriving soon for their meeting. Saying a quick prayer that Dave could follow the fast version, Lexi began to fill him in on the bombshell assignment that landed in her lap a fortnight ago. She confided in him about the fear of failing her Bachelor if she didn't pull it off - and the very real possibility of choosing a new major. Exhausted, Lexi slumped back in her seat eager to hear Dave's advice.

"Would your University accept a youth event with our church as your assessment?" Dave asked after a long moment of silence. Lexi lifted a shoulder. "I'm not sure, I'll ask. Why's that?"

"Well, Pastor Walker and I were speaking about the annual springtime fundraiser, and we threw around some ideas. But I'm thinking about handballing it to you for your University requirements."

Eyes widening, Lexi considered Dave's suggestion just as Dylan's bike could be heard rumbling into the driveway. Not long to discuss it. "Ok, sure. Yeah, I'd love to organize something for the church's fundraiser!"

Dave opened his notebook and pulled out a list. "Here is the list of ideas we were throwing around. I am partial to the concert idea. If you choose to go down the concert path, I have a friend in the States who is a booking agent for some pretty big gigs." Dave left the sentence hang. Lexi tore her eyes from the list of awesome fundraising ideas and smiled at Dave.

"I like concert idea, too," she said.

"I'll go grab his card for you," Dave said as he rose and hurried into his library just as the doorbell chimed. Mind illuminated with possibilities, Lexi rose to answer the door while tucking the list of ideas into her back pocket. Worries eased, Lexi wished she'd spoken up sooner. It had been so easy, and now she felt great! With a beaming smile, she opened the door to her friends. Lightened in spirit, she joined in the meeting with new energy and joined in the laughter as they planned a great Friday night service for the youth.

ELEVEN

*W*ith a hand laying over her stomach, Lexi strode towards the double doors of the church hall and glanced up at the star-filled night sky. "Ok, Lord. You want me on this team? You show me where I fit in, ok? Ok." With a nod, Lexi closed the distance to the hall. She was determined to face her fears, trusting that God had it covered. The sound of the heavy door closing behind her echoed loudly through the room, and she jumped, affirming her level of nervousness. After sucking in a deep breath, Lexi squared her shoulders and tossed her hair before crossing the hall to where Dave was sitting with Trent and Nick. "Evening fellas, where's the others?"

The three men, undisturbed by her seemingly noisy entrance, looked up at her from where they lounged on the stage. "Hey Lex, they'll be here soon," Nick said, turning his attention back to a notepad sitting between the three men. "They're familiar with the game we're playing, so they don't need the refresher."

Climbing onto the stage, Lexi scooted over to the boys and listened as Dave went through the game rules again. Lexi laughed when he handed her a glowing halo prop. She turned it over in her hands. "What do I do with this? You didn't mention this at our meeting."

Trent snatched it and put it on Lexi's head. "What do you think you do with it?" he asked, chuckling.

"You wear it to identify yourself in the game, Lexi," Dave said. "You and Hope are the guardian angels." Slapping a headband with flashing red horns on Trent's head, Dave rose. "Trent and Dylan are the Grogs. Nick, you're the referee."

The hall door closed loudly, and Lexi jumped again as Nick groaned. "Come on Dave, I don't want to stand on the stage during the game, the game doesn't need a Ref."

Watching as Dave met Dylan and Hope in the middle of the hall and hand them their props, Lexi heard Nick groan again and turned to him. "Surely it won't be that bad. Why do you have an issue with it?"

"Ignore him. Nick's just annoyed because he won't be in the action," Dylan said, coming to lean against the stage, horn headband hooked onto his belt. "Regardless of what he thinks, the game does need a Ref. Who else would be in charge of the lighting? Or give direction to kids who might get lost in the dark?"

Dave came alongside Dylan, his presence effectively silencing Nick's rebuttal. "Ok team, are we all clear? When the youth arrive, I'll split them into two teams: Hope and Trent are playing inside with one group; Dylan and Lexi you're outside with the other group. Nick, you stay onstage and make yourself visible in case anybody needs you. I'll signal you when to kill the lights. Ready?"

As if answering Dave's question, the hall doors opened again, and the first of the youth entered - filling the quiet expanse instantly with noisy chatter and high-pitched laughter. With a quick leap off the stage, Hope went with Dave to greet the youth, while Nick and Trent began moving couches and the whiteboard into the wings. Suddenly unsure, Lexi reached for Dylan's arm before he could move away. As if reading her expression, Dylan leaned back casually against the stage, not drawing any attention to them and waited.

Lexi took a breath. "I think I've just forgotten what I have to do."

Using his finger, Dylan drew on the stage as he went over the game again. "Ok, you represent a guardian angel. Your job is to protect your team while they search for the flashlight - which represents Jesus - that's hidden in the church gardens. I represent a devil. And my job is to get in the kid's way and try and stop them from finding the flashlight. If I catch one of your team players, they are frozen and can no longer play until unfrozen by you. Once your team finds the flashlight, they then need to find me. If they manage to capture me in the flashlight's beam before time's run out: you've won. But, if I freeze all your players before the time runs out . . ."

"You win. Yep, got it," Lexi said, watching the youth spread out over the hall. "It's going to be hard to play in the dark though."
Dylan tapped the horns hanging off his belt. "That's why these are illuminated. There are lanterns set up outside for us and fairy lights inside for the other group. Don't worry, you'll be fine."

Reassured by Dylan's explanation, Lexi stood with him while Dave addressed the growing crowd of youth and split them into teams. Lexi noticed Dylan was gone once her team was lined up behind her, and she flicked a confused glance across the hall at Hope. At Hope's nod toward the side doors, she realized that Trent was also gone - the boys had left to hide for the game.

Lexi closed her eyes and said a quick prayer, blinking them open just in time for Nick to plunge the hall into darkness. Excited squeals erupted as both teams began shuffling from the hall and toward their game areas. Once her eyes adjusted to the darkness, Lexi could see the lanterns Dylan had mentioned and was thankful for their soft light. Then she noticed her team surrounding her, and Lexi froze. Her mouth dried up as she looked from one shadowy figure to the next. When she opened her mouth to speak, Lexi snapped it shut again – suddenly aware that she had no idea what to say. Their restlessness grew, and she noted the glances a few were throwing over their shoulders. Panic began to prick the back of Lexi's neck as she searched her mind for some instruction to give them. "We n . . . need to find the light. So, um, let's ch . . . check out the ga . . . ga . . . gardens by the shed."

Whispers of approval quickly rippled quietly amongst the group before they darted off, disappearing into the darkness. Frightened to let them out of her sight, Lexi ran sluggishly after them. When she saw Dylan's illuminated headgear near the shed, she urged herself silently forward, realizing the youth hadn't seen him in their eagerness to find the flashlight. And she'd sent them straight to him!

Suddenly, a shriek pierced the night air, and Lexi pulled up short. Adrenaline burst inside her, kicking her system into action as she sprinted towards the shed. Motionless silhouettes littered the playing field, and she aimed herself at them, as another scream echoed across the lawn. Whipping her head around to make sure Dylan wasn't nearby, she went to task unfreezing her team. One by one, as they ran off to rejoin the game, Lexi began to feel a strange sensation settle over her, causing her skin to prickle. It was too quiet. "That was too easy," she mused. Dismissing the thought as her imagination shifted into overdrive, Lexi took off after her team. She gasped loudly as Dylan stepped into her line of vision. The dull red light from the horns he wore cast eerie shadows over his face as he stood before her, poised, eyes unblinking. Her breath came in short puffs as she faced off with him; her whole body electrified. He would catch her if she tried to run, but she had to run. Her team needed her! A challenging expression formed on Dylan's face, and she saw him tense as she considered her only option.

With uncharacteristic boldness, Lexi lunged forward, throwing her body weight to the right, then to the left. Dylan's chest felt like a wall and his arms like a vice as her charge came to an abrupt end. Writhing in his hold as her team called for her, Lexi increased her struggle to break free as a chuckle emanated somewhere deep inside the chest behind her. Frustrated, she growled. Unable to catch her breath, Lexi opened her mouth to demand he let her go when a beam of light suddenly danced across the lawn toward them. Dylan's arms fell away as the light grazed over them, and Lexi whirled around to see his retreating silhouette suddenly illuminated by light. With a triumphant laugh as her team raced past and encircled him, Lexi approached him with a feeling of confidence.

Dylan sunk to his knees, defeated. There was something about the way he was kneeling before her with his hands clasped behind his head, which caused Lexi to smile. She reached out and pulled the headband from his head, and Dylan rolled his eyes. "Yeah, well done, Lex. Beginners luck," he teased.

TWELVE

With a happy sigh, Lexi switched on the kettle and continued putting away the lunchtime dishes. She was still flying after the excitement of youth group last night. The sensation of confidence remained, and Lexi felt she could face anything and come out on top. She led a group of youth to win a game! She did! On her own. The kettle boiled and she began making herself a cup of tea when her phone buzzed on the countertop. *"Come for a drive with me? Brad."*

Her gasp filled the empty room, and she covered her mouth while staring at the text message. How did Brad get her phone number?

"Everything ok?"

Lexi nodded then looked up at her Mum. "Oh yeah, fine. I thought you left for the shops?"

Mrs. Slaydon crossed the room to the coffee table, lifted her purse, then turned to leave the room once more. "I got to the end of the street and realized I'd forgotten my purse. Sure everything is ok, sweetie? You look flushed."

Lexi nodded again and watched her mum continue from the room. Leaning against the counter, Lexi read the message again. How did Brad get her number? Lost in thought, Lexi took her bottom lip between her teeth. The only person who connected them was her brother. And knowing his feelings about Brad, she couldn't rationalize him giving over her number, but who else was there? With shaky fingers Lexi hit reply. A door slammed in the house, and she jumped. Stashing the phone under a tea cloth, Lexi returned to her cup of tea. Frowning, she looked at the crumpled tea cloth. Why did she feel the need to hide her phone?

"Sis, you in here?" Shaun strode into the room as she took a sip from her drink. He looked over the open living and dining area, eyes coming to rest on her in the galley kitchen. "Are you doing anything?"

Lexi lifted her mug to him as she swallowed the bergamot and citrus infused liquid, nodding her head. Met with a dismissive look, she watched as Shaun took a seat at the counter.

"Well, when life slows down a bit for you there, want to shoot a few hoops with me? I've got the basketball semi's this week and need to get in a bit of practice."

Lexi's phone buzzed under the tea cloth, and she lunged for it, drawing a suspicious expression from her brother. A blush flooded her face as she pocketed the phone. "I suppose I could give you an hour or so practice time." He raised an eyebrow, eyes flickering to the crumpled tea cloth. "Just an hour?"

Her fingers itched to reply to Brad's message, and her mind wanted to know if he was the author of the newest message. "Well, I have homework to get through and a major assessment to work on. You play 'A grade,' why do you think you need more than an hour?"

"Why can't you give me more than an hour?"

"For reasons I just said!" As soon as the lie crossed her lips, Lexi hated herself. Aware of Shaun's scrutinizing frown, she dunked the tea bag a couple of times and took a deep breath to settle herself.

Shaun held her gaze a moment before rising. "I think I'll ask Troy for a hand. He needs to work on his defense anyway. See ya."

Her breath rushed out as her brother left the room, and Lexi felt the cold fingers of guilt delve into her mind. Unable to relax, Lexi pushed off the bench and took off after Shaun – her intention to reveal what she had hidden. Then her phone buzzed again. Lexi paused in the hallway, her attention returning to Brad. Withdrawing the phone from her pocket, Lexi read the messages from Hope and felt frustration nip at her. Closing Hope's request for a shopping trip, Lexi opened Brad's message. And before her courage faltered, agreed to his request.

* * * *

"Where are we going?" Lexi said through a fit of laughter, clutching at the bandana covering her eyes.

Brad laughed loudly. "Quiet down you. You'll see. Just another hour or four to go."

"Brad!" Lexi slapped at his leg and fell silent when she felt his fingers curl around hers; his lips pressed into her palm moments later, and her body warmed.

"I'm only joking. Another twenty minutes. You're not getting car sick over there are you?"

She shook her head. "N . . . no. I feel fine. I'm so excited!" As they drove, Lexi tried to use her available senses of smell and hearing to try and identify where they might be. She leaned toward her open window and listened to the sounds outside the car, while a CD started to play - its bass beat vibrating through the car seats and the foot well, as the male singer's rugged voice belted out one of her favorite songs. She grinned at Brad, remembering his phone's ring tone the first time they met. "So, you like Bon Jovi too?"

"Only been to every concert they've had."

Brad's hand wrapped around hers as they listened to the words of the songs. And Lexi couldn't keep the smile from her face. The air was becoming fresh as they drove, and taking in a deep breath, she caught the scent of eucalyptus, wet bark, and fresh rain. As they went around another bend, she turned to Brad. "Are we in the mountains?"

Brad scoffed, "You have no idea."

Still smiling out her window when Brad pulled the car to a stop, Lexi listened as he opened and closed his door. She heard the muffled crunching sound as he walked outside, then the sound of her door opening. A light breeze blew into the car, bringing with it a stronger scent of the smells she had picked up earlier. The laughter of children echoed. She frowned.

"Well are you getting out?" came Brad's voice. Unsure where he was, Lexi held out her hand. She swung her legs out and stood up when Brad took her hand. The crunch beneath her feet told her the ground was stony, but the sweet saltiness of the ocean confused her even more. She giggled nervously. "I have no idea where we are."

"Yeah! I know. Come on."

A light breeze blew, and Lexi held down her white cotton skirt as Brad led her across the crunching stones. Coming to a stop, he turned Lexi and gently pushed her into a seated position. Her perch rocked gently, and she heard a chain snap into place. A ripple of anxiety fluttered in her stomach. "Brad?!'

"I'm here. Don't panic." The seat moved again as he sat next to her and the sound of a chain clicking in place sounded again. Feeling his arm come around her, Lexi nestled into his side and ignored the unsettling feeling curling in her stomach. Suddenly the seat lurched, and they were moving slowly uphill. Her stomach dropped as she realized there was nothing under her feet anymore. Panic began to tap on her mind, and gripping her seat, she turned to Brad. Then his mouth settled upon hers. His kiss deepened as he cupped the nape of her neck, and she heard wolf whistles somewhere below her. The bandanna came loose, and he drew back. Missing his contact already, it took Lexi a moment for her peripheral vision to register the trees and ocean stretching out around them. Blinking, she looked past Brad. It was twilight over the bay, and the water rippled like liquid gold under the crescent moon. The lights of the city twinkled in the distance - the view was breathtaking! Treetops beneath and beside her were waving gently in the evening breeze, as were the red chair seats suspended by a cable in front and behind them. Slowly they made their way up the side of the mountain. Lexi had never seen anything so beautiful. She returned her gaze to Brad once more, and his roughened hands enclosed her face. Softly his kiss fell upon her lips once more.

*   *   *   *

The gentle clink of their glasses echoed in the small private room overlooking the blackened bay - highlighted by the city lights and a long, thin sliver of moonlight reaching across the waters to the shore. No longer able to withhold her curiosity, Lexi replaced her glass on the wooden table. "How did you get my number, Brad?"

The flickering candle between them illuminated his dark eyes, revealing their delicate hazel color with a dark ring around their edge. "Off Shaun," he said, gathering up her hand. "Lexi, I hope you don't mind, but there is something I'd like to get off my chest."

Unsure, she moistened her lips. "Ok, sure. What is it?" Never having seen a man nervous before, she wondered if that was what he felt as his Adam's apple bobbed in the lengthening silence.

"Look, I know you're unsure. And I know your brother wouldn't agree if you said yes, but I would really like to date you."

Further questions about her phone number vanished. Thoughts of Brad's earlier kisses renewed in her mind, her body responded, and she couldn't breathe, let alone speak through the heaviness she felt. Though aware of a subtle warning deep in her conscience, the delicious feelings flooding her system seemed to block rational thought.

"Lexi?" Brad's thumb brushed the back of her hand.

The slightest movement from him caused an avalanche of emotion, and her breath caught. A vague caution flashed again within her conscience, and Lexi flicked her eyes back to his. She couldn't put her finger on it, but something felt . . . dubious. Brad was beside her in a heartbeat, and the sensation of his hand curving around the nape of her neck drowned any resistance. Knowing he was going to kiss her, and helpless as his fingers tangled in her hair, Lexi forgot her misgivings. She watched the smile playing upon his lips as he leaned in; teasing.

"Say yes," Brad whispered.

Lexi's hand twisted into his shirt as she looked back at him. The other boys she'd been out with didn't make her feel this way, but that didn't mean it was wrong. Perhaps the others just weren't right. She dipped her head once; his kiss wasting no time accepting her unspoken answer.

THIRTEEN

"Hope. Call me back, I have big news!" Ending the call, Lexi strode toward her afternoon classes. Thankful that she had a firm grasp on the unit content, Lexi allowed her mind to wander as she doodled on a notepad. Leadership meeting was later in the evening, and for the first time since it commenced, Lexi was looking forward to it. A smile tickled her lips as her mind drifted to Brad, and Lexi blushed hotly as the memory of being in his arms came back to her. Just the thought of him electrified Lexi and set her pulse racing.

One problem stood in the way: Shaun. Hiding her new boyfriend from Shaun also meant hiding the relationship from her parents. Still, there was something in Brad's casual dismissal of how he got her number. Curious, Lexi chewed her pen cap. She would ask him again the next time they spoke - if she could keep her thoughts in order while in his company.

Her phone buzzed on the desk, and Lexi grinned broadly, noticing that it was from Hope. She would tell Hope, and maybe the boys, about Brad after the Leadership meeting. Handouts passed over her desk, drawing Lexi from her daydreams. Taking one, she passed the rest on, and Lexi tried to tame the nervous butterflies that bounced around in her stomach. The discussion of her major assessment with the professor was up next. When class was dismissed, Lexi collected her books and filed out with the other students.

Lexi mentally went over her pitch once more, praying she'd be allowed to bring the proposal to life. The room was large and imposing, Lexi anxiously observed. Nervously, she waited by the Professors desk for their appointment. Bookcases reaching to the ceiling captured Lexi's attention, and she wondered about the books on the uppermost shelves. When were they last read?

"Miss Slaydon, thank you for coming in."

Lexi's pulse jumped as the wayward thoughts of ancient books dashed from her mind. She rose from her chair to greet the professor, and lightheadedness left Lexi wishing she'd stayed seated. As he approached, the professor gestured for her to sit. He also appeared large and imposing, and Lexi swallowed hard as she retook her seat. "Thank you for seeing me, sir."

He sat heavily in the high back leather chair and checked his watch before looking over his glasses at her. "What is it you would like to do for the year's major assessment, Lexi?"

His voice seemed to echo around her, and Lexi felt fear tapping her on the shoulder. If she gave way to the sensation coming over her, the meeting would be over, and she couldn't let that happen. Lexi shuffled forward in her seat and forced her mind past the threatening panic. "Sir, I wish to plan and conduct a concert for the youth at church. It will double as our major annual fundraiser for mission work. I've discussed the assessment requirements with my Youth Minister, and we believe this will satisfy the objective." As soon as the last word passed her lips, the room fell silent. And panic tried to ensnare Lexi once more. While the professor considered her proposal, Lexi picked at imaginary lint on her cardigan sleeve. Then she focused on the rhythmic cadence of her breathing to keep her mind distracted. The silence was uncomfortable, and after what seemed like minutes, she heard him clear his throat, and Lexi looked up.

The professor wore a pleasant expression as he wrote on the notepad. "Ok Lexi, I've made a couple of notes and find no issue with your idea. You may proceed, and I look forward to your presentation." The professor rose, indicating the conclusion of their meeting, and she followed suit - surprised at how quick the dreaded encounter was over.

When he offered his hand, Lexi took it firmly. "Th . . . thank you, sir. I'll do my best."

* * * *

Half walking, half skipping, Lexi made her way down the strip towards the Beach-Side Hotel, eager to catch up with her friends and tell them her big news. It was a cool night with a biting wind, and she glanced upward. Moonlit cumulonimbus clouds gathered above, and Lexi wrinkled her nose at them. Winter was settling in - the season she'd happily do without. Answering the summons of the unexpected group message from Nick, Lexi hurried her pace - anticipating what he had to share.

The hotel was crowded. "Odd for midweek," Lexi thought as she picked her way through the milling people and out to the beer garden. A roaring fireplace in the lounge was the apparent draw for many of the patrons. Stepping around the last of the crowd, Lexi pushed through the frosted glass doors leading into the beer garden and crossed the floor to join her friend.

Nick lowered his glass as Lexi approached. "Knew you'd be early."

Smiling at Nick's comment, Lexi perched on a stool and glanced around. "Couldn't get a seat by the fire instead?"

He shook his head and took a sip from his drink. "I hope this will be enough for you," Nick said, inclining his head to the small chiminea burning nearby. She shuffled her seat closer to it just as the beer garden doors swung open behind her.

"So, whose news are we here to hear?"

Hope's comment made Lexi laughed, and she swiveled on her stool to greet her. "Nick's. Mine can wait."

Nick looked at her. "You have news, too?"

The door swung open again before Lexi could answer, and glancing over, she saw Trent and Dylan enter – each carrying a tray of drinks.

"Right, what are we celebrating Nick?" Dylan asked, placing the tray on the table.

"It better be good; it's freezing out here," Trent said, taking a seat next to Hope and tossing bags of chips onto the table.

Nick raised a hand for attention. "Well, apparently Lexi's got news too, and where I come from it is ladies first. So, Lexi?"

All eyes instantly fell upon her, and she nodded, forcing herself to meet each friend's curious gaze. If she had to do a presentation in a few months, what better audience to practice with than friends? The chiminea's heat was beginning to radiate through her clothing, and she shrugged the coat off her shoulders. "Actually, I have two pieces of news. First one is, the church's annual fundraiser this year is going to be a concert, and I'm sort of running it as an assessment for Uni. And, the second is . . ." Lexi caught her breath, a smile taking over her face. "I have a boyfriend."

Hope squealed as the boys asked in unison, "Who?!" Before she could explain, Hope grabbed her arm. "Brad?" "The guy we played pool with?" Nick asked.

Lexi laughed as she answered "yes" to both questions. Then she felt Hope's grasp intensify.

"I need details!" Hope squealed, her brown eyes flashing with joy.

Ignoring the murmurs of disinterest from the boys, Lexi filled Hope in on what had happened since the last time they saw each other. With a promise for more details later, Lexi cut the conversation with Hope short and threw the discussion back to Nick. "Wait just a moment," Dylan said. "What's the go with this concert you mentioned?"

Conscious of already taking up some of Nick's planned evening, Lexi shook her head at Dylan's inquiry. "That can wait. Nick, tell us your news now!" Nick drained his drink and dug his hand into the bowl of peanuts. Lexi knew he was drawing them out, and she crossed her legs - foot bouncing impatiently.

Eventually, Nick cleared his throat and pushed the bowl of peanuts back. "Well, I've passed my physicals, and I'm off to the Academy. I leave in two weeks."

Jaw dropping, Lexi stared at Nick. "W . . . well, how long will you be gone?"

A smile broke the nonchalant expression he wore, and Nick reached for another drink. "Just three months. I'll be back in time to see this big fella take home the best and fairest for the year." Dylan chuckled at the compliment directed at him. "I'll be back before you know it, guys. I just ask that you keep me in your prayers. I'd like to score a posting at a nearby station after I graduate.

I really don't want to be sent far from The Valley. Particularly not to a city precinct!"

As Nick turned to address a question from Trent, Lexi turned her attention to Hope's insistent tapping on her leg.

Hope mouthed the words: "Surprise party."

Stifling a giggle, Lexi nodded at Hope's suggestion. Then she focused on the boy's conversation, only to find Nick glaring at them. Lexi raised an eyebrow at him as she flipped her palm up, "What?"

"I saw that look you two! I know you're up to something."

"Or plan to be up to something," Dylan said, interrupting Nick as he replaced his drink on the table.

Sharing a giggle with Hope, Lexi plucked a chip from the bowl and popped it in her mouth. "Guess you'll just have to wait and see."

FOURTEEN

*L*exi sat on the edge of her bed, gasping through her silent giggles. The way Brad spoke of life at the work site had Lexi in tears – the laughter making her stomach ache. A few deep breaths later, she stood. Conscious of the time, she placed her phone on speaker and began to apply light make-up for the night. "So, are you coming along to help out this week?"

Any time she asked Brad to join her at youth group, he always had a reason why he was unavailable - work commitments, his age, or family issues. Lexi explained again that Dave welcomed extra adults for added supervision, although, in truth, Lexi had been thankful for Brad's absence. It allowed her to concentrate on her new position, but Lexi also wanted to share the experience with him. The feeling that he'd gone cold on the idea since they'd been together disappointed her a little.

Brad cleared his throat. "Well actually, now that you ask - I was going to surprise you by turning up."

Lexi paused, staring at her shocked reflection in the mirror. A smile slowly appeared on her face. "You serious?"

His rugged chuckle came down the line, creating a starburst of excitement in her stomach. "Yes, I'm serious. See you at 7:00 p.m." The line went dead and a long moment passed before Lexi squealed in excitement.

A few happy hops and a quick wardrobe change later, Lexi grabbed her church bag and flew down the stairs. Time in the car on her way to youth group was generally spent revisiting the plan the team created earlier in the week, but Lexi couldn't concentrate. Excited and eager to see Brad, Lexi turned the radio up and sang at the top of her voice until rounding the corner leading to the church. Enthusiasm restrained, and radio turned down, Lexi turned into the car park.

Brad's white, classic XYGT was parked out front, and he was leaning against the driver's side door talking to Trent. She pulled into the space next to him and caught sight of Trent wave before he disappeared into the hall. "Hi, you," Lexi said, stepping from her Jeep as Brad pushed off his car and moved towards her.

He stopped just in front of Lexi and took her hands, entwining his fingers with hers. "Hi yourself. Big night planned?"

Lexi tipped her chin as she smiled at him. Brad had a way of making her feel fabulous just by being in his company. "We always have a big night planned. You should come along more often."

Brad's eyes twinkled in the car park's low light, and she caught the corner of his mouth hitch up as he stepped in closer.

"Ok team, gather 'round. Where's Lexi?" Dave's question about her whereabouts stole her attention from Brad, and she glanced over her shoulder towards the hallway doors.

Light spilled out the open doors, and Lexi heard Trent's muffled voice answer: "She's outside."

Lexi turned back to Brad. He gave a slow nod and moved to step back, but Lexi took his hand and led him inside. "I'm here;

I'm here!" Lexi called as she released Brad's hand and trotted over to the gathered Leadership Team.

The night was theirs to run as Pastor Walker was away, leaving them in charge. Dave had given them their roles for the evening at their meeting Monday night, and it was up to them to pull it off. Thankful he had given her a support role for the games and then café duty afterward, Lexi forced her mind to focus. Closing herself in the huddle with her friends, she forgot about the hall filling with youth - and her boyfriend, who was looking more awkward with each passing minute. After a quick prayer, Dave disbanded the huddle, and Lexi turned toward Brad. At least until a hand hooked her elbow, turning her around.

"Where you going?" Hope asked. "We need to get backstage."

With a glance at Brad, Lexi saw Nick toss him a basketball. Hope sighed, and Lexi looked back at her. "What?"

"Brad will be fine, sweetie. He's a big boy. Let's go."

Lexi knew Hope wasn't going to listen to any attempted negotiations, so she allowed herself to be half dragged backstage to work the props. The night went quickly, and Dave upheld his promise – for which Lexi was thankful. She tidied up quietly while the youth gathered in the hall for the evening message. Once she'd finished putting things away behind the stage, Lexi slipped back into the hall to listen to Dave's teaching.

"Don't get too comfortable; we're on café duty."

Looking up at Dylan, Lexi found him leaning against the wall - his manner unhurried. It was a bit early for café duty, but with a shrug, Lexi rose and nudged him towards the café. Once the doors had swung closed behind them, she let out a long breath. Then Lexi looked around to see what needed to be done first.

"While you were cleaning up backstage, I came out here and got things ready to go," Dylan said.

Sitting up on the island bench, Lexi swept the fringe out of her eyes. "I see that. So why did we need to come out now? I wanted to hear Dave's message."

Dylan sat at the serving counter, and Lexi sensed there was something he wanted to say. Squinting at him, Lexi crossed her arms and was about to ask for his thoughts when the café door swung open.

Hope entered, looking around the room. "Is Dylan in here?"

Lexi looked from Hope to Dylan as he rose from the stool, and Lexi jumped off the bench, not sure if she should say anything. "It's a bit early for café. Can we steal Dylan for a moment?" Hope asked.

Lifting a shoulder, Lexi nodded her head. "Sure. Can I do anything?"

As Dylan slipped from the room, Hope shook her head. "No, everything's fine, hun. We'll be right back." As the door shut behind her friend, Lexi raised an eyebrow. Something was up. She stared at the door a moment longer before deciding to make herself a drink while she waited. Too much moving around distracted the youth while Dave was speaking, so Lexi chose to stay in the café. The door swung open again, and Trent entered. "Lexi, you got a sec?"

"Sure, what's up? Is Brad ok?"

"Yeah, he's fine. Dave's about to run through an impromptu game, and he'd like us all out in the hall while he explains it."

A frown flickered across Lexi's brow as she moved toward Trent. It was unusual for Dave to run an unplanned event. As she followed Trent out into the hall, her eyes fell upon Dylan, Hope, and Nick as they stood with three of the five small groups that had been formed. Trent moved to stand with one of the remaining groups while signaling her to move to the last. A familiar sensation curled in Lexi's stomach as she moved toward the group waiting for her. Dave's voice became a drone as Lexi looked around the room, her heart pounding inside her chest. The sight of Brad standing in Nick's team brought a whisper of a smile to her lips, before noticing the way he was taking in the room – and her. His expression was dark.

". . . fifteen minutes guys, and I'll see you back here for the banquet!"

All of a sudden, four of the teams stampeded from the hall in loud confusion, leaving Lexi and her team behind. The youth were eager for direction, and bodies fidgeted with excitement as they waited for Lexi. She swallowed hard and moistened her lips. She knew she had fifteen minutes, but didn't know what for. Suddenly the youngest in her team was tugging her arm and pulling her towards the kitchen, the rest following. Alarmed, Lexi allowed herself to be led. When the doors swung shut behind her, Lexi found the courage to ask what was going on.

"It's a challenge, Lexi," Ruth said. "Each team has fifteen minutes to create something for the banquet. The envelope tells us what we are supposed to make."

Hands shaking and mind whirling, Lexi received the envelope and opened it. *Team four: Cake.* From the piece of paper in her hands to the ready faces in front of her, Lexi looked around the room. She took a step back, leaned against the bench tops and looked at the note again. "Why would Dave do this?" Lexi groaned under her breath. Then, her head snapped up at a sudden thought. A five-minute mud cake! She hadn't made five-minute mud cakes in a long time, but the recipe flashed in her mind. With a sense of urgency, Lexi grabbed the apron hanging behind the door. Whatever Dave was up to, she wouldn't let it ruin the evening for the young people on her team.

Lexi's voice echoed sharp and clear when she called for the required ingredients. Once they were before her, she expertly mixed several single-serve cakes in coffee cups and slipped them into the microwave. While the first batch was cooking, Lexi called her team around the island bench and gave them all a mug. Quickly she showed them how to make the five-minute mud cake: two minutes to prepare, three minutes to cook.

When the microwave pinged, Lexi directed half of her team to withdraw the mugs and put the new ones inside. With a quick glance at her watch, Lexi informed the team they had seven minutes to go. Enthusiastically, Lexi encouraged her team as they tipped out the mug-shaped mud cakes onto plates and began decorating them. Nervous energy filled the kitchen as they all worked to complete the task. Lexi was so wired and happy that she felt ready to burst. Situations like this would normally cause panic! Why was she happy?

As the microwave pinged again, and the last of the mud cakes went in to be cooked, she showed the youth how to put the cakes together to create one large centerpiece cake. With a quick check of her watch, Lexi discovered they only had three minutes remaining. Calling the youth to place all used mugs in the dishwasher and wipe down the bench, she retrieved the last of the mud cakes from the microwave and placed them delicately around the display they had created. After sprinkling a light dusting of icing sugar over their masterpiece, Lexi stood back to admire their work of art. A siren rang out in the hall, declaring that time was up. The banquet had begun.

With careful steps, Lexi carried the tray with their team's creation into the hall and watched as the other teams re-entered - Trent and Dylan's from side doors, Nick's from behind the stage, and Hope's from the main entrance. Curious to know what the other teams had to do, she watched each carefully. Dylan's team was hanging handmade paper lanterns, and Trent's team was arranging table decorations. Hope skipped toward the table with her team, the group filling glasses with what looked like lemonade made from the church's lemon trees. And Nick stood nearby with his team, watching. After placing their cake on the table, Lexi looked at Nick curiously as she tried to figure out what he'd done with his team. Grinning, Nick shoved his hands into his jean pockets.

"Welcome to the banquet!" Dave called out from the stage. "Enjoy."

No sooner had the words left Dave's mouth, then the youth raced to the table. The hall filled with their animated voices and laughter while they sampled the simple banquet before them. Walking quietly along the back wall Lexi came to a stop beside Nick.

"So, um, I can't figure it out. What did you guys make?"

"Garments," he said. "Have a closer look. I wasn't overly creative, but it was the best I could do in fifteen minutes."

With a more critical eye, Lexi looked over his team and began to notice they did look a little odd. She raised an eyebrow and turned back to Nick. "Did you raid the youth's stage wardrobe?"

He grinned. "Well, what would you have done?"

"Hey, guys," Dave said quietly, joining them. "I'm impressed. Really impressed. It was a spur of the moment idea that fell in line with my talk on the banquet waiting for us in heaven, and you all brought it. Especially you Lexi."

Dipping her head as her friends echoed Dave's kudos, Lexi remembered the sensation of fear that morphed into a feeling of joy at the outcome. It was strange but liberating. And she couldn't explain it. It had never happened before. "That was sneaky Dave, it nearly killed me," Lexi answered him.

His gaze fixed on her as he let the silence grow. "But it didn't, did it?"

"No, I guess it didn't." Lexi smiled back at him as Hope embraced her. "Thank God!"

FIFTEEN

"*I* don't care how it turned out, Lexi! That's not the point!"

Lexi blinked. "Um, why are you so angry?"

"Because he should know better. He should have more respect for you!"

Open mouthed, Lexi forced her mind to process what was happening. Brad's attention was focused on the road as he drove them to Nick's for the surprise party she and Hope had organized. Brad had been fine when he picked her up. Then she'd asked if he'd had fun at youth group the previous night, and his rant against Dave had started. In an effort to restore peace, Lexi explained that the night ended well, so no harm done; still, Brad didn't want to hear it. She looked out the window and bit her lip, this was uncharted territory.

"Look, I'm sorry for yelling. I just can't believe you'd defend the man when he put you into a situation you're terrified of - after *promising* he wouldn't."

Unable to deny the reason behind Brad's annoyance, but wanting the topic dropped, Lexi laid a hand upon his arm. "I can see what you're saying, and I'll talk to Dave about it."

"Tonight," Brad said. His face was like stone in the dim evening light, and she instantly read the this-conversation-is-over look.

Lexi nodded her head slowly. "O . . . ok. At some stage, I'll see if I can have a word with him."

Brad continued to stare ahead as if she'd not spoken, and the fluttering in her stomach intensified. Nick's surprise party - albeit thrown together quickly - was something she was looking forward to. And having an argument with her new boyfriend on the way to the party irritated her. Lexi didn't agree with what Dave did, but she felt as though she could understand his reasoning. Certainly, she couldn't deny how happy it made her - knowing she could succeed despite her fears! Just the memory of it brought a slight smile to her face as she looked out the window. Feeling Brad's hand on her leg, she turned to him.

He glanced at her before returning his attention back to the road. "Thanks."

The party was in set up mode when they arrived. Dylan and Hope were hanging fairy lights around the house. Haphazard music sounded while Trent tried to get the DJ system programmed. Lexi directed Brad toward the parking area, then waved to Hope.

Hope jumped off the veranda and jogged over to them. "Hi, guys! Lex, did you bring the stuff?"

"I did!" Lexi said. Once out of the car, she hurried to open the passenger side door and pulled out two freezer bags. She handed one to Hope, one to Brad, and then reached into the car to retrieve the third. "Ok, show me to the kitchen." Everything she'd requested had been laid out and set-up. She looked at Hope with a thankful grin. "You are so organized!"

"That was Dylan. He was here before I arrived. Ok, I'll leave you to it. See you on the dance floor."

As Hope danced from the room to the rhythm Trent had pulsating through the house, Lexi reached for the cream and electric beaters sitting on the bench. "You want to go see what the boys are up to, or watch me beat cream?" Lexi asked Brad as she turned the beaters on. Flicking a glance at Brad, she saw him make a disinterested face as he looked around the room.

"Nar, I think I'll go see what Trent's up to," Brad said as he headed for the door.

Lexi watched him leave, her instinct buzzing that he still wasn't happy – with her, or Dave, she wasn't 100% sure – but she wasn't going to let it ruin the night. Nick was going to love and possibly hate this. She smiled to herself, switching off the beaters.

"C'mon, what's the joke?" Dylan asked.

Looking over her shoulder, Lexi giggled. "Oh, just thinking about Nick at the Academy, and the fact he'll not see another dessert for three months."

Dylan came alongside her, and she smiled at him before returning her attention to the desserts. With expert hands, she smothered the Pavlova's in cream and decorated them with cut up fruit. Once they were finished, Lexi moved them to the side and decorated the white chocolate mini cheesecakes with blueberries and chocolate flakes.

Dylan chuckled quietly, "He's going to hate you for this you know?"

"He'll love me more though," Lexi said, placing the desserts on the serving trays before turning to face him. "So, what brings you in here? I keep getting this feeling you want to talk about something."

The corner of Dylan's mouth hitched up as he rested a hip against the counter. "What makes you think that?" Lexi raised an eyebrow in answer as she tilted her head.

Dylan chuckled as he linked his hands around the back of his neck. "Ok. The thing is, my football captain, Andrew, is retiring from The Valley Tigers after this season, and I'm being considered to take his place as captain next year. And, while I would love the opportunity, there is Jack to think about."

Lexi nodded. Dylan's younger brother, Jack, was troubled. Lexi did not know the boy well, but she was aware that the death of their father three years ago changed Dylan's brother. Just hearing about Jack's rebellious nature was tiring - let alone living with the guy! She understood Dylan's concern and slumped against the counter in thought. Acting as Captain for the town's local Football Club would require a lot of Dylan, and caring for Jack was a balancing act. "Have you prayed about it?"

Dylan dipped his head. "Many times."

Lexi let her breath out. She knew all about waiting for answers to prayers; it was an exercise in faith and patience. "When will you find out if you have the job?"

His hands slipped from the back of his neck and hung off the "Paid in Full" dog tags he wore. "After the Vote Count," Dylan replied, ruing the three month wait.

To encourage him, Lexi leaned forward and rested a hand on his arm. She hoped her words wouldn't sound like a cliché or patronizing. "Well, I guess you have three more months to pray. Trust that God will make things clear to you when the time is right. He wouldn't ask you to do anything that would negatively impact you or your family. He always wants the best for us. You know that, right?"

Dylan's grin turned wry as he looked back at her. "Yeah . . ."

A throat clearing drew her attention to the doorway, and Lexi saw Brad leaning against the door frame eyeing her and Dylan. His arms were crossed, and a muscle worked in his jaw. Her hand fell away from Dylan's arm as she smiled at Brad while gesturing for him to come in - though Brad remained where he was. "Dave's free for a chat, if you're not too busy, that is."

Lexi's brow flickered as she caught Dylan stretch to his full 6 foot 5 inches. The insinuation in Brad's words was plain, and

Dylan didn't like it either. "Thanks, Brad. I'll pop these desserts in the fridge and be right out."

Brad remained where he was, watching her closely. The tension was thick as Lexi picked up a tray and moved to the fridge. Her earlier irritation reignited as she moved the second tray to the fridge. Brad's bad mood and rudeness were concerning. With the food in order, Lexi flicked a glance at Dylan, and left the kitchen with Brad at her heels. Dave was waiting for her seated under a tree bedecked with fairy lights. Eager to get the bogus conversation out of the way, Lexi sat down while Brad hovered nearby.

"I hear you'd like to have a chat about last night, Lexi."

Her smile felt unnatural. "Um, I just wanted to make sure that, you know . . . in the future . . . that I'm not put on the spot again." Unable to look at the youth minister, Lexi dropped her eyes from Dave's. Feeling like a bug under a microscope, Lexi toyed with her bracelet. As Dave's silence lengthened, Lexi lifted her eyes to him and caught the slow dip of his head that told her he knew what was behind their conversation.

"Lexi, I understand it was a challenge that made you uncomfortable, to begin with, and I thank you for having the courage to come and speak with me about it."

Suddenly, the house behind them was plunged into darkness, and the music ceased - creating an eerie quiet. The fairy lights in the tree above them continued to flicker. Lexi stood as the front door banged opened and a male silhouette appeared on the porch. "Dave? Lexi? You guys out here?"

"We'll be in shortly, Trent," Dave said.

"How far away is Nick?" Lexi asked, rising from her seat.

"He's about three minutes away."

As the door closed behind him, Dave rose and cleared his throat. "We all cool?"

Lexi caught Brad's eyes and taking his hand, nodded her head. "Thanks so much for having a chat with me about last night "

"My door is always open, Lexi," Dave said, turning to move back inside. "Now, let's go give Nick one memorable send off to the Academy."

As they headed back towards the house, Lexi glanced up at Brad. "So, are you happy now?" she asked in a soft teasing tone, desperate for the tension to ease.

Brad sniffed, his fingers loose in her grasp. "He was careful with his answer, that's what I heard."

Her mouth tipped, sure that a hint of levity had returned to his voice, and Lexi hurried him up the front steps. Quiet as field mice they slipped into the darkened home to await Nick's arrival. Lexi waited behind the couch, anxious to see Nick's reaction to their surprise. To her knowledge, Nick had no idea what they were planning. Music was ready, food was ready, and they were all together.

When Nick approached the darkened house, Lexi held her breath. Her fingers dug into the soft plush of the sofa as she knelt behind it, and her muscles twitched. All her nerves tingled, and she felt like a ball of energy just waiting to explode! Any minute now! Just wait until he opened the door.

The door opened and Lexi's "SURPRISE" shout, caught in her throat. She could hear murmuring. As her eyes adjusted to the dark, she could see Nick's hand was raised up to his ear. The other hand dropped a bag onto the floor, then his car keys onto the coffee table. He was on the phone! She tapped Dylan on the shoulder, and he moved in close. "You're going to have to turn on the lights. Pretty sure he's not . . ."

"Nar," Dylan whispered. "Let's listen to his conversation."

Suddenly, a blinding light filled her vision. Lexi flinched as people began jumping out from their hiding places and shouting "SURPRISE!" The music burst into life at a deafening pitch, and once she regained her senses, Lexi stood to join the crowd. She lent her voice to the welcome only to find Nick calm and standing still in the middle of the chaos.

A smile broke out over his face as he ended the phone call and waved down all the noise. Hands lowered, postures sunk, and the music scratched to a halt. "Guys, guys, guys! That was an important call."

Momentary silence filled the room, and Lexi could see the doubt that flickered in exchanged glances. Then those closest to Nick rushed at him, and the music boomed back into life. She shook her head. So like Nick to pull a counter-prank! While Nick circulated, Lexi joined Hope in pushing couches and chairs out of the way to prepare a dance floor. Nothing could dim the smile on Lexi's face as she listened to those around her grow louder and louder with each 'Nick' story told. The laughter that followed made her heart swell.

Lexi picked up a large floor lamp and looked around for a safe place to put it. When a hand fell on her shoulder, Lexi spun around.

"You!" Nick said. "I knew you and Hope were up to no good." His eyes were shining and that grin of his, slow and confident, curled up on one side of his face.

Lexi laughed and put the floor lamp down. "Of course. Did you honestly expect anything less?"

He leaned in. "I've seen the kitchen too, by the way, . . . that's below the belt."

"Ahh, you love it!" Lexi said, her laugh catching in her throat as a wave of emotion rolled over her. All of a sudden it hit her - Nick was leaving for three months! What would she do without him? He was such an important part of their team. Impulsively, she wrapped Nick in her arms. "Yeah, well, just make sure you come back to us, ok."

"I'll be back before you know it," he said as his arms enfolded her. "Just keep me in your prayers." Lexi felt a lump form in her throat. "Always."

SIXTEEN

*R*unning her hands over her hair, Lexi forced her breath out as she slouched back into her seat. Ideas for the concert had dried up, and she was only two hours into the scheduled four-hour program. The pressure was on, as there was just a week remaining to complete her proposal. Distractedly, Lexi tilted her mug and wrinkled her nose seeing it was empty. Perhaps a tea break would refresh her and clear her thoughts.

The house was quiet. Just the billow of the chiffon curtains and the sound of her soft footfalls over the tiled living room floor tickled her ears. As she passed the hallway leading towards the front door, shadowy figures caught her attention, and she doubled back. "What are you guys doing here? And can't you knock?"

Laughter preceded Hope and Trent into the living area, and Lexi smiled to herself as she switched the kettle on. Waving a mug over her shoulder, she questioned, "Tea?"

"Hot chocolate for me, honey," Hope said.

Trent shook his head, holding up a sports drink.

Lexi listened as her friends explained their unexpected visit while she finished preparing the drinks. With the task complete, she headed back outside and motioned for them to follow. Lexi placed Hope's drink on the table and nestled back into her chair to sip her tea. Still amazed at how they banded together to help her with the concert prep, Lexi knew that they would come up with a way to end the night. Clinging to faith, Lexi issued a silent prayer for the ability to pull it off.

*　　*　　*　　*

Hours later, the outdoor table was strewn with exhausted cups of tea, hot chocolate, jugs of water, and plates encrusted with crumbs. The floor nearby was dotted with balls of screwed up paper. Proud of what they had achieved, Lexi stretched her arms above her head, tossed her pen onto the pad in front of her, and grinned at her friends. "Guys, I could not have worked this out without your help."

Hope yawned, belatedly covering her mouth with the back of her hand. Moments later the patio doors opened, and Shaun stepped out. Trent stood and reached over the table to shake Shaun's hand as Hope straightened up in her seat.

Lexi grinned at her friend before she looked over at her brother. "Hey bro, what's up?"

Shaun looked preoccupied, and Lexi sat up, gesturing for him to sit and join them. He ignored her and looking over the table, dipped his head at Hope, then turned and went back inside.

Frowning, Lexi looked after him.

"What's up with him?" came Hope's query from behind her.

Fingers of trouble tickled her, and Lexi turned back to her friends, "I'm not sure." Just then, her phone buzzed with a message from Brad. She swallowed, sensing the two were connected somehow.

"You ok, Lex? You've gone a shade paler." Trent commented.

Had Shaun found out about her relationship with Brad? A hand on her knee broke into her thoughts, and Lexi looked up.

Hope was staring at her, her eyes searching. "Sweets, did you even hear Trent? What's going on? Is Brad ok?"

Looking over the table and their notes concerning the concert, Lexi wished they could stay in the peaceful, brainstorming mode, but she knew that was over. Something was up. She opened her phone and read the message from Brad: *Hey beautiful, give us a call.*

Shaun and I have been talking. Brad x

Pulse jumping, Lexi closed her phone and looked at her friends. Moistening her lips, she tried to calm herself. "Ah, well. Um, Shaun doesn't want me to see Brad, but I've been seeing him anyway. And I think Shaun just found out." Silence fell over them, and Lexi closed her eyes. How could such a great morning plummet so fast?

Trent rose from his seat. "I think Hope and I should get going so you can talk to your brother."

Lexi rose reluctantly. Trent was right. As they walked to the front door, Lexi thanked them for helping with her project. After a few laughs and hugs from them both, she felt ready to confront Shaun. Not a moment after the door closed, Lexi heard Shaun say her name. Turning, she found him stepping up to the landing from the sunken lounge, his face like an approaching storm. She swallowed.

"Sis," he quietly said, eyes unblinking. "Are you seeing Brad McCormick?" She nodded once, and Shaun's reaction was felt rather than heard.

Shaun blinked slowly and took a long breath through his nose.

Lexi braced herself for the moment that the calm façade broke and he began yelling at her. But when Shaun looked at her again, she saw concern in his eyes.

Shaun cleared his throat. "How long?"

His casual manner unnerved her. Lexi was sure she could feel a hatred simmering under the surface – something she sensed would be unleashed if she answered one of his questions wrong. "Officially, maybe a month."

Shaun's face began to distort. "And, how long before that?!"

She bit her lip. "Maybe a month."

"Why haven't you told anybody? What's the secret?" "Well, I guess I didn't . . ." she stuttered. "How did this come about anyway?"

Blinking, Lexi moistened her lips. Perhaps the second question was more vital to him and the first no longer needed answering? Thankful, as she had no answer for it anyway, Lexi replied with what she did know. "He messaged me, asking me out on a date."

"Where did he get your number?"

Lexi closed her eyes and took a moment to compose herself. She knew Shaun was on edge, but it didn't excuse his rudeness. With a quick prayer for patience, she opened her eyes as the last thing Shaun said came back to her. "What?! *You* gave him my number!"

The calm façade broke as Shaun crossed the floor and stopped inches from Lexi, his fists planted on his hips. "I *what*?"

Brad's story and the question of its truthfulness began to fill her mind as Lexi took in the fierceness of her brother's eyes, the thin line his mouth had become, and the flare of his nostrils. Suddenly unsure, her voice was a whisper when she spoke. "H . . . he told me you g . . . gave it to him."

Shaun was gone before the last word left her mouth. His shoulder brushed hers in his haste, and she spun around to stop him.

Lexi's hand collided with the closing door, and she growled as she shook her hand out. Hot tears sprang to her eyes. She had to call Brad! Running down the hall to retrieve her phone from the patio table, she wiped her eyes while blaming herself for not speaking up earlier. Brad's story about getting her number had been suspect, and instead of following her instinct, she ignored it. Stupid! Lexi tossed chair pillows, papers, and the empty jug in her effort to find the phone. As the jug clattered to the ground, Lexi ran both hands through her hair. When the house phone began to ring inside, she ignored it and continued her manic search. Until she heard Shaun's voice. Racing inside, she realized he was speaking through the answering machine.

" . . . guess by now you are looking for your phone. Well, stop looking. Because I have it. We'll talk when I get home."

The message ended, and she jumped as the phone was slammed down. The wind rushed from her lungs, and she sat down at the kitchen bench, her arms limp by her side. Feeling alone and vulnerable, Lexi felt tears spring to her eyes again as prayers for her brother and boyfriend raced through her mind.

SEVENTEEN

The muffled sound of the front door closing echoed through the house. Facing her bedroom door, Lexi waited for Shaun to walk through it at any moment. Self-pity had vanished in the long, quiet hours she had been alone, and in its place was annoyance. How dare he try to hold control over her, or try to enforce who she was allowed to go out with – wasn't she an adult? Couldn't she make her own decisions? She growled again, her breathing shortened as she waited. No one appeared, but she heard the lounge room TV switch on. It wouldn't be their parents, as they were away for the weekend. No, Shaun was home and expected her to join him.

Stubbornness locked her jaw, and she crossed her legs. However, the return of her phone and a need to know what Shaun's interference had wrought launched Lexi out of her seat.

Shaun glanced at Lexi as she entered the room, then he returned his attention to the TV. He seemed calm and in one piece.

Lexi considered asking what happened, but a sudden need to see Brad flooded her system. With a calming breath, she stepped down into the lounge and stopped near Shaun. "Can I have my phone back please?"

"He's playing you, sis. Just like I said he was." Shaun tossed the phone to her without looking away from the TV. "But hey, by all means, go and see him. You won't take my word for it? So, find out for yourself."

Lexi caught the phone against her chest, and she glared at her brother. She hesitated a moment, then decided against discussing it and turned on her heel to run to her car. An urgency to see Brad increased with each heartbeat, so she had to go.

When Brad didn't answer after her second knock, Lexi felt worry nip at her mind. His polished car was in the driveway, where was he? She stepped off the front landing and pulled out her phone to call him. But the rattle of a latch drew her attention back to the front door. A gasp escaped her mouth as Brad appeared and she darted over to him. "What happened?!"

Pain marked Brad's features as he gestured for quiet. Taking her hand, Brad led her inside. He shut the door quietly behind her as she entered, then he moved past her into the living room. "Sorry beautiful, I have a bit of a headache - as you can probably tell."

Lexi closed the distance between them and stopped before him. The blood stain on his shirt, red stain under his nose, and shadows over his cheek told her all she needed to know. And Lexi shook her head. Did her brother really beat up her boyfriend? She felt as if she'd been winded. Laying her fingertips to his marked face, she watched as Brad gently took hold of her wrist and lowered her hand. He shook his head before sinking down onto the couch. The room's curtains were drawn, shrouding them in shadows, and the air was stuffy. Sensing darkness that wasn't due to the drawn curtains, Lexi shifted her weight, unsure of what to do. Brad groaned from the futon couch, and Lexi took a seat beside him. Laying a hand on his thigh, Lexi watched as he laid back against the pillows. "Can I get you anything for your headache? A glass of water maybe?" He closed his eyes, then took hold of her hand.

"Brad, I'm so sorry. Shaun took my phone, and I couldn't let you know he was on his way." He didn't answer, and Lexi felt her pulse jump. Was he mad at her? She inched closer, "How did Shaun find out anyway? I never told him we were seeing each other."

Brad opened an eye; his voice rasping when he spoke. "I suggested he, Renee, you and I could go see a movie on the weekend and he laughed. I guess he thought I was making a joke. Anyway, he left the work yard shortly after. Next time I saw him was when I opened my door. He let himself in, then gave me this." Pointing to his eye, Brad sniffed, "I don't think we should see each other anymore. I don't want to cause trouble for you and your brother."

Laying a hand on Brad's chest, Lexi leaned into him. "Who I see is not Shaun's decision." Surprising herself with the purr in her voice as she sought to reassure, she grinned at the playful expression that lit Brad's eyes. When his hand slid up her neck and into her hair, Lexi allowed him to pull her forward and kiss her. Long moments passed before she felt him loosen his hold on her, and not wanting to be apart, she slipped in beside him on the couch. Lexi loved the feeling of his arm around her. His heart beat strong and steady under her palm, and she found herself wondering what it was about him that Shaun found so appalling. Why did he hate him so much? He was nothing but kind and considerate to her, protective, respectful . . .

"Babe?"

Looking up at Brad, Lexi gave him her attention. "Yeah?"

"I've been thinking about that night at youth group, and I still can't get my head around what Dave did to you. And I *really* didn't like how he fobbed you off at Nick's." Brad started to push himself up, and Lexi scooted backward. He winced, and she held her breath as he closed his eyes for a moment. When he opened his eyes, Lexi felt her stomach lurch at the pain behind them. "I keep seeing you white as a ghost that night. You looked like a rabbit in the crosshairs."

"Brad, it's ok."

"No!" he said, as a roughened hand cupped her face. "Lexi, it worries me that you want to be around these people."

A warning flashed through her mind at his words, too fast to grasp. Brad's hand slipped from her face as he pushed himself up and moved with measured steps to the kitchen. Not knowing what to do, Lexi followed him. As she passed through the doorway from the lounge to the kitchen, she paused after spotting him in the adjacent laundry. Brad pulled the shirt off his back and dropped it in the trough. Lexi had guessed what his form was like, but seeing it uncovered was something else. The muscles in his arms and back held her attention as he scrubbed the blood stain from his shirt, and Lexi caught her lower lip between her teeth. When he glanced over his shoulder, she blushed and turned away, feeling embarrassed by her open admiration of him. Moments later she heard the laundry door close.

"What's up?" he asked.

Lexi continued to look out the window over the kitchen sink. Shirtless, Brad was almost too intimidating for her to handle, and there was a heaviness in her limbs whenever he was around that made her feel like she couldn't stand up. She giggled nervously, sensing him drawing near. "I . . . I've forgotten what I wanted to say actually."

He hummed as if in thought, and a thrill ran through her body moments before feeling his arms come around her. Her breath caught sharply feeling his body press into her back. "Let's see if I can help you remember."

The uneven tone in his voice and his closeness sent her mind into overdrive. Lexi felt her muscles start to tremble, and she closed her eyes. "It's . . . it's really not important."

Brad's lips pressed into the curve of her neck, and she grasped the kitchen counter. "I think..." His voice was teasing against her neck, and her body ran hot as he spoke against her ear. "...you were going to ask why it worries me that you want to be around certain people."

She couldn't think, but she nodded inadvertently. Pressure applied to her hip compelled Lexi to face him. Unable to look at him, Lexi averted her face, but Brad tipped her chin back to him for a kiss. Capturing Lexi's hands behind her back in one of his, Brad cupped the back of her head. Brad drew back unexpectedly, and Lexi blinked. She felt as if she was getting her sea legs as she watched him step back from her and rest a hip against the opposite counter.

"It worries me because I know you're going to get hurt if you continue to hang around them."

Lexi gripped the bench behind her as the room continued to sway. She needed her brain to kick back into action if he was after a conversation. "Huh?"

Brad crossed his arms. "C'mon, Lexi. You take behavior and psychology as core subjects, you should know this stuff! I shouldn't have to point this out to you."

Sensing the seriousness of the conversation, the fog in her mind began to lift, and she cleared her throat. What Brad said was true, but she trusted Dave.

"I get it, you trust the guy," Brad went on. "But you told me you went to Dave's home and had a face to face conversation with him. You told him about what scares you and why you weren't keen to take on the role. So, it's not like Dave didn't know what he was doing."

"Brad, I don't believe that's what . . ."

"What is it then? He rolled the dice and gambled with the outcome. Gambled on your response. What if it backfired?"

A new tension began to fill the room, making Lexi uncomfortable. Anger clouded Brad's concern for her, and his tone didn't match what he was saying. "Brad, I think that Dave was allowing me to show myself. He was encouraging me to do what I thought I couldn't. Does that make sense?" she asked softly, wanting him to relax.

"What if it backfired? What about the concert? All this time you've spent trying to mentally prepare yourself for that moment . . ."

Lexi took a step towards him. "Well it's better to drop the ball in front of a small, friendly group than in an auditorium filled with strangers, isn't it?"

"You're not thinking about this properly," Brad said, linking his hands behind his head. "Which is concerning, since it's what you hope to direct your future toward." His torso was powerful and his gaze steady as he looked back at her. And Lexi suddenly wondered if his shift in body language was a calculated move. Something said she should leave and think about this in the quiet of her own room - somewhere without the sound of her heart beating in her ears or his perfect muscles to distract her.

Brad stepped toward her, and she involuntarily took a step back as his arms enfolded her waist. His mouth hitched up in an impish grin. "I'm sorry. It's not you that I'm annoyed with. It just hurts me to see you walked over and pushed into things you don't want to do. I care about you, Lexi. A lot."

Relaxing, though still unsure where to put her hands on his perfect physique, Lexi kept her arms tucked into her chest and grinned up at him. "Yeah?"

"Yeah."

She bit her lip through a smile.

He rocked her gently, playfully, as his eyes took on a gleam. "So, this isn't much of a hug with your arms tucked in like that." She giggled and knew she was blushing, when he took one of her arms and laid it behind his head, then did the same with the other before holding her against him. She could hardly breathe past their closeness. "I know you want to help out because that's just the beautiful person you are," Brad said, then kissed her lightly on the nose. "But you can only do what you can do and feel comfortable with. Maybe you can be an assistant or something in the background? Promise me that you'll re-think this Leadership Team thing and look after yourself."

Brad finished his sentence with a lingering kiss, leaving her mind fuzzy. An unfamiliar yearning tugged at Lexi. When he pulled his head back to look at her, Lexi smiled slowly.

"How about on Monday you tell Dave that you quit."

Her mind suddenly cleared like a strong wind had just blown through, and she pulled back. With clear vision, Lexi watched him closely and ignored the thrill pulsating through her body. "But I enjoy being part of the Leadership Team. I don't want to quit."

A subtle hardness covered his expression at her reply, and Lexi wasn't surprised when Brad's arms fell away. He stepped back. "Ok," Brad replied. "I don't agree, but I'll respect your decision. Please respect mine when I say I won't be coming back to offer help at youth group while you're on the Leadership Team."

The air rushed out of Lexi's lungs, and she stared open-mouthed at him. Something wasn't adding up, and she couldn't think straight. She needed to go. Needed to think! Unable to keep the sadness and confusion from her eyes, she searched for the words to say.

Clearing his throat, Brad said them for her. "You need to go, huh?"

Nodding once, Lexi headed for the door - Shaun's words playing over and over in her mind.

EIGHTEEN

"*M*aybe he's genuinely worried about you?" Hope said. "I was also a bit surprised at Dave putting you on the spot like that."

Lexi shook her head. "No. It was more than that. I just can't put my finger on it." Sitting in the change room as Hope hung up the discarded pile of clothing, Lexi filled Hope in on what had happened since the last time they saw each other. She crossed her legs, and her foot bounced in agitation. To recap her conversation with Brad and what he expected just irritated Lexi the more she reflected. Did Brad think she was going to give up? She sighed. "Are you sure it's ok for me to sit in here while you're working?"

"Sure! As long as I keep getting this pile of clothing down, my manager won't care."

Restless, Lexi stood and paced. "You know that feeling when something isn't right?"

Hope chuckled, folding a blouse. "Yes, I do."

Stopping in front of the bench Hope was working at, Lexi frowned. "I like him a lot. A lot! But I'm not going to quit just because he's asked me to! What am I? Some submissive thing he can say 'jump' and I'll ask how high?"

Hope grinned as Lexi began pacing again; then she pulled another bin of discarded clothes over to hang up.

"You know what," Lexi said, stopping again in front of Hope's work station. "I think I'll talk to Dave about stepping up in the group a bit more. You know, give me the opening prayer, or a chance to run the ice breaker. It can be practice before running the concert." She started pacing again. Something was tapping on her mind. Lexi felt close to understanding, but she couldn't grasp it. "There is some ulterior motive in him asking me to quit. Or, do I sound paranoid? I mean, Brad's body language was calculated to intimidate."

Hope chuckled again, "Maybe a little bit paranoid. But I always say 'go with your gut.' If you're feeling something is off, it most likely is."

The warning in Hope's words was noted, and Lexi nodded. She would be careful with Brad – she *had* to be – but she was also going to prove him wrong. Shouldering her bag, she waved goodbye to Hope and strode from the store. Her next stop? To see Dave.

* * * *

"Lexi. Wasn't expecting to see you today."

"Hi Dave," Lexi said, stepping past the man into his home. "I need to have a quick chat. Am I interrupting anything?"

"Not at all, come in, and have a seat. You're not working?"

"I took the week off to get ready for the concert this weekend and study for upcoming exams," Lexi spoke while following Dave to the kitchen. She took a seat at the table, then waited until

Dave joined her. After taking a deep breath, Lexi filled him in on the happenings that led her to their unexpected discussion.

Dave listened with interest, but when she stated the reason for their impromptu meeting, he sat back in his chair, crossed his arms, and eyed her critically.

Unsure, Lexi timidly grinned back at him.

"So, let me get this straight." Dave cleared his throat. "You want me to give you a leading rotation this Friday evening, so you can prove to your boyfriend, who won't be there, that you can do what he says you can't. And that is how you intend to justify remaining a part of the Leadership Team?"

Lexi felt her smile fade as she considered Dave's summary. Is that what she'd said? Avoiding his gaze, Lexi studied the cornices of Dave's home while thinking it over. Realization broke like the dawn, and she had to be honest with herself: that is what she'd said - just with less padding. Her shoulders slumped, and Lexi felt Dave lay a reassuring hand on her shoulder.

"Lexi, if you want to step up in this role, be sure it's for reasons between you and God - not to prove your boyfriend wrong. I admire your willingness, but the motivation and intentions are wrong, I'm sorry to say."

Although she knew Dave was right, she still felt an eagerness to at least *try*. No sooner had the thought entered her mind than Dave pushed his chair back and stood.

"The concert is Saturday night. That will be a great platform for you to step up in, if you wish. See how you do with that, and if you still want to step it up at youth group, we can talk more about it then. How's that sound?" The kettle boiled and Dave began making their drinks.

He was right. While she waited, Lexi's eye fell upon a new print hanging in the lounge. She narrowed her eyes, trying to read it from where she sat in the kitchen. Unable to make it out, Lexi rose and walked over to it. *"Those who trust in themselves are fools, but those who walk in wisdom are kept safe. Proverbs 28:26."*

"Powerful, isn't it?" Dave said, coming alongside her. She took the drink he offered and blew at the steam rising off the chocolate colored liquid.

"You could say that. I feel I've been suitably rebuked." Dave chuckled, and Lexi turned to him. "I'm serious."

"I know you are," Dave said, shifting his gaze from the artwork to Lexi. "I bought that print today."

Silence hung over them as Lexi looked back at her Youth Minister. Her path was suddenly clear, but she couldn't put it into words. She just knew. She was to step out in faith.

Dave put his mug down on the nearby coffee table. "You ok?"

Lexi nodded. "Yeah, I'm good."

"How about we take a seat? I'm keen to hear about how this concert is coming along."

The change in topic was just what she needed. Shifting gears, Lexi began to fill him in on the plans for Saturday night.

Dave's smile broadened the more she spoke, and her excitement for the upcoming event outshone Lexi's anxiety. When she addressed the evening's projected revenue, Lexi saw Dave's eyebrows reach for his hairline. And laughter bubbled out of her.

"How have you managed that?" Dave asked.

Lexi sat forward on her chair and gestured with her hands as she spoke. "I got a lot of help from Trent and Hope. We brainstormed, and Trent came up with selling raffle tickets. Hope is organizing a market to set up on the lawn area outside the stadium. I've kept the ticket prices low so more can attend, and the bands have even kept their booking fees low! I'm stunned at how it has all come together within the church's budget."

Dave's phone rang, interrupting their conversation. Lexi motioned for Dave to answer it, then reached for her drink. Surprised at how excited she was becoming about the concert, she found herself wishing it closer. Unable to contain her smile, Lexi bowed her head and thanked God. Quietly she prayed that her enthusiasm would not be swamped by anxiety. Then she addressed the uncertainty she felt about completing the follow-up presentation for her Uni class. As Dave took the call into his library, Lexi toyed with her empty mug, thinking of the week ahead. It was going to be a big one, and not just with the lead up to the concert. There was the matter with her brother to address, and her mood shifted with the thought. Shoulders slumped, Lexi whispered, "God? I need you."

* * * *

"Honey, is that you?"

Lexi paused in the foyer of the family home. Her head fell back against her shoulders, and she groaned after hearing her mum calling from the kitchen. All she wanted to do was lay on her bed with a book after the day she'd had. She needed to zone out. She sighed. "Yeah, it's me, Mum."

"Could you come to the kitchen, please?"

Lexi's brow furrowed. Her Mum sounded different, not like herself at all. Lexi called out she was coming and headed to the kitchen. As she stepped into the open living area, Lexi found her parents and Shaun - seated at the kitchen table. A lump lodged in her throat, closing her airways, and Lexi knew by the heat filling her face that she was revealing the very thing she was trying to hide - guilt.

Her Dad rose as she approached. "Think we need to have a talk, young lady."

Ooh! Dad used the 'young lady' term. Lexi felt her heart gear up a notch as she lowered herself into the seat her Dad gestured to. Who would ask about Brad first? As her Dad took his seat again, her mum seemed nervous, and Shaun wouldn't look at her. Lexi felt like she was on trial.

Mr. Slaydon cleared his throat. "Lexi, Shaun tells us you're seeing a young man from his workplace. A man that he has made explicitly clear you are to stay away from." Mr. Slaydon paused.

"Why then have you decided to start up a relationship with the man? And why keep it a secret from the entire household? That's not the behavior I would expect of you."

Lexi couldn't deny anything her Dad said, and she brushed the fringe out of her eyes. Shrugging, she said, "I don't know. I mean, I met Brad before I knew he worked for Shaun. And I hoped Brad would ask me out. When I found out he was one of Shaun's co-workers? Well, he was already, sort of, courting me: coming to the café, inviting me to picnics on the beach . . ."

Shaun stood, his chair scraping on the tiled floor. "That's his game, Lexi, and you're falling for it! He's known all along who you are!"

"Shaun, sit down."

Looking at her Dad's calm, but stern expression as he addressed Shaun, Lexi spotted her brother's pacing in her peripheral vision. "Dad, Shaun's adamant that Brad is up to no good, but I . . ."

"How'd he get your number then? Tell them that story." Shaun said, ceasing his pacing.

Open mouthed, Lexi stared at her brother, surprised at how he was attacking her. She stood. "Maybe I will after you've told them how you gave Brad a black eye!"

Shaun recoiled, "I didn't hit him!"

Lexi felt her eyes flash. "Oh, what? He hit himself did he?"

Mr. Slaydon stood. "Little children, sit! Now!"

Lexi sat immediately and watched Shaun lower himself back into his seat. When their Dad used *that* tone, they were no longer adults. Instead, their behavior marked them as little children, and a sentence was about to be handed down. The room fell quiet, and Lexi picked at her fingers - unsure if she should say anything.

Mr. Slaydon cleared his throat again, and she looked up. "Lexi, I am very disappointed in your behavior. However, you are old enough to choose who to date for yourself. Having said that, you understand then, that any repercussions from this relationship, are on your head?"

She nodded. Just agreeing with her Dad made it seem like she'd sentenced herself. Did she really want to go down this path? Lexi bit her lip.

"Shaun," Mr. Slaydon continued. "It is normal for a brother to be on guard with any man dating his sister, but you need to cool it. Lexi has heard your concerns and has chosen to continue the relationship. You, . . . we all need to respect that. Are we clear?"

Flicking a glance at Shaun, Lexi saw him dip his head once, then roll his eyes as he looked away.

"Lexi?"

Worried about what her father was going to say now, Lexi looked back at her Dad and found his expression had darkened a shade. "I better not hear of any more secrets, young lady. We've raised you better than that, and we expect your respect. Clear?"

Guilt sat like a stone in her gut. "Yes, sir."

Mr. Slaydon stood. "Good then. This conversation is over."

As the room emptied, Lexi sat at the table while the silence around her spoke volumes. Long moments passed before she rose and left the dining area. Concert plans demanded her attention.

NINETEEN

The day of the concert was upon Lexi sooner than she anticipated. Tension was still high in the family home, giving her a dose of insomnia. And, knowing Brad wasn't at Youth Group last night because of her felt like a physical slap. Lexi sighed loudly as she pulled into the car park of The Valley's Entertainment Complex and killed the engine. She had to snap out of the mood she was in if she was going to nail the evening ahead, but she couldn't even muster a prayer; she was that tired – physically and emotionally. With another heavy sigh, Lexi shouldered her bag, and after locking up her Jeep, headed towards the complex. Her phone vibrated, and she pulled it out of her bag. Lexi saw a message from Brad on the screen; a whisper of a smile appeared on her face as she read his message. He would be arriving soon, and a hug from him was just what she needed. Suddenly the Center's double doors burst open, and Zac Porter, the churches resident IT guru stumbled through into the car park. Breathless. "Lexi, thank the Lord you're here! The bands need to do final sound checks, and my computer with the evening program on it has just crashed! Have you got your laptop on you?"

Breaking into a run, Lexi called out to him that she had her laptop in the bag, and Zac turned and darted back into the complex. With force she'd never used before, Lexi ripped the door open and ran after Zac towards the bird's nest. Once beside him, Lexi handed him her laptop and let him go to work, anxiously biting her nails behind him. The CB crackled into life, and Zac handed it over his shoulder to her without breaking concentration on his task. She took the CB and listened to Scott backstage bark out requests and found her system buzz into life. Affirming she had received the message, she handed the CB back to Zac and made her way backstage.

Filled with strange adrenaline, Lexi strode through the auditorium towards the stage, leaped up the side stage stairs, and flipped the stage curtains aside. As the heavy drapes swished back in to place behind her, Lexi took in the crazy whirl around her. The room reminded her of an ant's nest with its fast-paced activity. People rushing; hurried chatter; nervous laughter. Suddenly her attention was captured by several familiar faces. Open mouthed she looked on in wonder, as long admired artists engaged with the backstage crew, weaving in and out of props, setting their equipment up . . .

"Lexi..."

Looking sharply toward the whispering voice, Lexi laughed. Scott stood beside her and looked at all the activity. "Pinch me." She said, "This has to be a dream."

His speech faltered, "Ah, if it was a dream, we wouldn't have issues."

Blissful state shattered, Lexi turned to Scott. "What?!"

Scott tapped a pen on his clipboard while he listed the setbacks they'd encountered, then looked at her with expectation. The CB crackled to life on his belt, and he turned from her as he answered it. Turning away herself, Lexi retreated into prayer. God would not have brought them this far only to see all their hard work fall apart at the last minute. "Ok, Lexi," Scott said, and she turned back to him. He hooked the CB on his belt once more and raised his eyebrows. "Our guardian angels must be at work! The lighting issues are resolved, and Zac's back online again in the bird's nest. All that remains is the trouble with the stage curtain not opening: I think the operating line is caught so I'll go up top to check it out. But I'll need a hand down here working the ropes from the tension pulley. You up for it?" Dusting off her hands fifteen minutes later, Lexi looked on as the magnificent magenta curtain swept closed without issue. Throwing a thumbs up to Scott, Lexi felt her stomach flip. The concert would start in just under an hour!

Needing a moment to herself, Lexi retreated to a quiet area backstage to practice her welcome. Luckily, she had prepared cue cards. With shaky hands, she pulled the cards out and began going over her speech. Suddenly a large black form dropped onto her cards from above. She squealed and tossed her cards as she jumped back. The form lay motionless over her scattered cards not five feet away! Shaking out the tremor in her hands, Lexi took a tentative step towards it. It didn't move. With unexpected boldness, Lexi stepped forward and nudged it with her foot. It was a toy. A toy spider! Lexi's mouth dropped open, and she took a long deep breath as she stared at the black, hairy toy. Then she threw a disgruntled glance at her cue cards laying all over the floor. Her breath shuddered as she released it, trying to keep herself calm when a chuckle sounded somewhere behind her, and she whirled around.

"It was just a gag, baby. Calm down a bit," Brad said as he pushed himself off the backstage wall and ambled towards her

Lexi felt her hands clench into fists, and her jaw locked as she watched Brad move towards her. There was no way to rationalize his thinking, and she wasn't sure she could trust whatever might fly out of her mouth.

He chuckled again, holding his hands up in a display of peace. "It was just a joke . . . thought I'd break your tension a bit with a surprise."

"With this?" She hissed, barely able to control herself at the thoughtlessness of his gesture. "You know I hate spiders!" The words caught in her throat, and her eyes began to feel hot. She shook out her hands and took another long, deep breath. A hug was what she needed - an encouraging word or the right bible text meant to inspire. Instead, Brad had frightened her! She began to shake. Nerves threatened her earlier calm, and Lexi stepped back from him, not wanting to create a scene.

Brad paused as a flicker of confusion tickled his brow.

On her knees re-organizing her cue cards, Lexi heard the auditorium filling just beyond the curtains. And, Lexi prayed earnestly that God would slow her racing heart and calm her breathing; she pleaded for His words of encouragement and assurance. Then Brad appeared on his knees next to her, gathering the cards that were out of her reach.

"Babe, I didn't mean to frighten you. I just wanted to ease some of your tension by making you laugh. I mean, I see how stressed you are; you're pale and shaking, and I'm worried about you." He paused, and Lexi felt his firm fingers curl under her jaw, turning her face toward him. His eyes were soft, his voice like velvet. "You don't need to put yourself through this, just say the word, and someone else will fill in and run the evening."

Taking a shaky breath, Lexi stood and immediately felt lightheaded as her peripheral vision blackened. Perhaps Brad was right, there was still time to get someone else. "Hey, Lex!"

Turning sluggishly toward the familiar voice, too engulfed in her sadness and fear of fainting to recognize who was calling her, Lexi saw a tall figure striding towards her. As her vision cleared, a weak smile played upon her lips as she recognized Dylan approaching. Noting that his stride wasn't slowing, Lexi stepped back. Moments later Dylan scooped her up in a hug and swung around. She laughed with surprise as her tension slipped away.

"You did it, Lex!" Dylan said, releasing her and acknowledging Brad with a dip of his head. "You should see how many people are out there! We're out of tickets, and it's standing room only now! I just wanted to find you and congratulate you. The evening's a success, and it hasn't even started yet!"

Never having seen Dylan so enthused, unless he was running out onto the footy field, Lexi had no words. Rather, she just smiled back at him. His face was luminous, and his blue eyes piercingly bright as he spoke. Then his gaze dropped to the jumbled cards in her hands. "What's that?" Dylan asked.

Lexi glanced down. "Oh, cue cards I made up to help me get through the night."

Dylan's countenance darkened; his voice lowered a notch. "You ok?"

A memory flashed through her mind. The things she felt she needed and prayed for moments before Dylan appeared - he'd brought all but one. She lifted a shoulder and tilted her head as she looked up at him. "You wouldn't happen to have a bible verse for me do you?"

He grinned, his answer as quick as the wink that accompanied it. "Philippians 4:13."

Surprised, laughter bubbled out of her. God heard her prayer and was with her! Grateful, she smiled up at her friend and thanked God for him. Hearing Brad clear his throat a little too loud next to her, Lexi glanced at him as Dylan began stepping backward. "Righto, kids. I better go sit in my seat before someone takes it. Catch you after the show!"

Nodding her head, Lexi watched as Dylan jogged from the stage and knew why he felt he needed to go. Brad. Another deep breath later, she looked at her watch - fifteen minutes until she was up. Surprised that a surge of nerves didn't hit her at that thought, Lexi felt a tingling of anticipation as the verse Dylan gave her flashed through her mind. *"I can do all things through Christ who strengthens me."* Filled with peace, she smiled and turned to Brad, "You better go to your seat too. I'll be backstage for the whole night, so I'll catch you afterward. I've put you next to Hope. Is that ok?"

Brad nodded coolly. Stepping closer to her he gave her a kiss on the cheek before heading out the same way Dylan had. Turning back to face her before disappearing behind the curtain, he wished her good luck. Then he flipped the curtain aside and vanished from sight.

As the curtain swished back into place, Lexi squared her shoulders and pocketed her cue cards. "Here we go."

TWENTY

The floodlights were piercingly white as Lexi slipped through the curtain and onto the stage. She squinted against their brilliance as applause rose like a roar and surrounded her. Lexi's stomach flipped, but not from nerves, and her skin tingled, but not from fright. It was that same feeling she'd felt at Youth the other week. A buzz of confidence! Shoulders squared, she walked towards the center of the stage and reached a steady hand for the microphone.

As she welcomed the audience with a clear voice and gave a short presentation on the church's fundraiser project for the year, Lexi felt as if she would burst. Her words flowed with inflection, even managing to draw a laugh or two from the audience. Lexi wrapped up her speech, and after introducing the first performance of the night, she exited the stage as the curtain lifted behind her.

Backstage, Lexi watched performance after performance. From her vantage point, she could see the bands and the audience; and, Lexi was sure this was what an out of body experience felt like. She'd never felt so free! There was nothing in her mind that overshadowed her enjoyment. If there were something that needed to be done right now, she'd step up and do it! Sure her feet weren't on the ground, she looked down. The gleam of the hardwood floors met her eyes, and she smiled. Yep. This was happening. Her number one fear had been faced head on and beaten! Overwhelmed, she turned away from the flashing lights, the swaying multitude, and the theatrics of performing bands. Needing a moment of silence, Lexi headed deep into the backstage area - somewhere out of sight so she could be alone with God. Finding an empty room backstage, where the base beat was nothing more than a dull thump, she closed herself in and gave thanks to God.

* * * *

Exhausted, Lexi slumped back against the locked entry doors of the Entertainment Complex and grinned at her friends.

"How you feeling?" Trent asked, handing her the keys he'd used to help lock up with. Lexi shook her head.

Still blown away by the evening and the conversations she'd had with long admired artists, Lexi was giddy with excitement and adrenaline. "Trent, I honestly don't know. The whole night has felt like a dream! God is good!"

"Sweetie, that was the best concert I've ever been too," Hope said matter-of-factly just as Brad and Dylan appeared in the foyer.

Brad slipped an arm around Lexi's waist, and then he tucked her into his side. "All the chairs are away babe, and . . ." ". . . and all lights are off," Dylan finished tossing her another set of keys.

"Alright then," Lexi nodded, "let's get going. I need some sleep!" Once outside in the cool of the evening, Lexi hugged each of her friends goodnight. After watching them drive away, she turned to Brad. "So, did you have a good night?"

A slow smile crept up on his face - a smile that turned her insides out. "I had a great night. And you, my girl, were amazing."

Thankful the dim lighting in the car park hid her embarrassment at his praise, Lexi giggled. "Thank you. I'm really happy you came. It meant a lot to me. Especially after hearing your feelings on several things earlier this week." A moment passed between them before Lexi dropped her eyes from his. The night had been so perfect she didn't want it to end. Lexi didn't want Brad to leave, and yet, the time had come for them to part again.

Brad stepped closer to her, hands deep in his pockets. "Why do you giggle?"

The warm evening breeze ruffled her hair, and she flicked the fringe out of her eyes as she looked back at him, trying to hold his gaze. "I don't know," she said. Not fully understanding why herself, but wanting to answer his question, Lexi tapped the side of her head and tried a teasing tone. "Just a lot of stuff going on up here at the moment." "Tell me about it," he said, closing the distance between them.

Although Brad's hands were still in his pockets, Lexi felt his touch by the way he looked at her, and she trembled. One thought dominated her mind at his nearness, and she recognized it shining back at her in his eyes. Daydreams and fantasies were made up of moments like this, and yet, she found herself wanting to flee. She frowned, shaking her head. Brad was her boyfriend! What was wrong with her? She took a step back.

"Need to get going, huh?"

"I really should, it's been a long day."

Brad took a long breath as he looked around the car park. "Ok, I'll follow you."

"You live the opposite direction from here, why would you do that?" Lexi asked, hugging her coat to herself as the wind picked up.

"I was raised to make sure your lady gets home after an evening out, so I'll follow you home."

The house was dark when Lexi pulled in the driveway - just a soft glow from the entryway lantern illuminated the front door. A quick glance in her rearview mirror revealed Brad pulling up along the curb, and she felt her stomach flip – she'd never heard of a guy following a girl to make sure she got home safely. Add gentleman to his list of growing qualities. As he made his way up the driveway towards her, Lexi stepped out of her car and looking up at the star-filled night sky and thanked God for the perfect night. "Looks like your folks have gone to bed."

Tearing her eyes away from the majesty of the Milky Way above, Lexi focused in on Brad moments before his arms encircled her waist.

"Good for us," he whispered.

Lexi tried to loosen his arms from around her waist. "Come on, I'm home safely now." His arms wouldn't budge. Instead, he leaned in and kissed her lightly.

"Do you have any idea how sexy you are?"

The unexpected compliment made her cough, then laugh. Composing herself, she looked back at Brad unable to keep the grin from her face.

Brad gazed back at her, seemingly unaffected by how his intended compliment was received. His eyes glimmered like the stars above, and Lexi found her resolve weakened with the knowledge that he'd meant what he said. His hold on her loosened as he withdrew an arm, and she felt his fingertips upon her cheek tracing her jaw.

"You are," Brad whispered. "Watching you on stage earlier was like watching a whole new side of you come alive. And let me tell you, there is nothing like confidence in a woman to tip her into being considered sexy."

Closing her eyes, Lexi's mind stuck on one word he'd used: confidence. The one thing she desired to be, and the one thing she'd envied in others. Tilting her head, Lexi looked back at Brad. "You think I'm . . . confident?"

Brad cupped the back of her head, restrained energy emanated from him, and she felt him press against her. 'Oh, yeah."

Catching her breath moments before he covered her mouth with his, Lexi allowed the sensation of being in his arms to catch her up and take her far away.

Long moments passed before Brad released her. Pressing his forehead to hers, he huskily said, "I'd love to stay the night, babe." "Brad," Lexi said, her voice breathy as she pushed him back a little - her mind divided.

"I can sleep on the couch," Brad offered. Capturing her hands, he cajoled, "I just don't want to be apart from you."

Lexi tugged her hands, but he held firm. "So this is why you wanted to follow me home? The truth comes out."

He chuckled, dropping his head momentarily. "Ah, maybe.'

She wanted to say "yes," but her conscious said "no." She'd not asked her parents first, and Lexi was sure Brad would be an unwelcome surprise after the things Shaun had told them. She smiled back at him. "Maybe another time."

Brad raised one of her hands to his lips and kissed it lightly. "Ok. See you tomorrow sometime?"

"I'm not sure," Lexi said haughtily. "I might make you do penitence after that stupid spider prank."

Pulled back into his arms, Lexi laughed happily as Brad chuckled pleas for forgiveness against her hair. Conquering her fear had left Lexi feeling lighthearted. She had placed 100% of her faith in God, and come out not only on top but feeling fabulous! She couldn't wait to deliver her presentation now and share what God had done. Dylan was right. She could do all things through Christ who strengthened her!

"What are you laughing at?" Brad asked, holding her close. "I'm just happy," Lexi said. "So happy."

TWENTY-ONE

*E*arly morning people generally aren't received warmly by those around them, but it never dampened Lexi's love of the morning hours. Everything was so fresh and new, and as Jesus said: "My mercies are new every morning." Yep, the morning was her favorite part of the day; however, heading to work on Monday, Lexi felt an extra touch of happiness lighting her spirit. The weekend concert seemed to have changed her perspective. For some reason, things that were once too big to climb over now seemed like stepping stones. God had answered her prayers. Full of energy, the spring in Lexi's step and happy greeting drew a glare from her workmate Michelle. As the girl tried in vain to reach a canister that had been placed too high for her 5'7" height, Lexi grasped it with no effort and handed it to her.

Speaking easily about their weekends, the morning past quickly, and before they were ready for it, they were inundated by customers on a morning tea break. Raucous laughter broke through the din of the packed Shopping Centre from a nearby table, causing Lexi to jump. She looked for the noisy customers and found them after following the trend of disapproving glares pointed in one direction. With a quick flick of her head, Lexi gestured for Michelle to have a look while she finished the drink she was working on.

"It's the guys from your brother's workplace," Michelle reported back. "About six of them sitting at a table by the window." A buzz zipped through her body at the thought that Brad might be stopping in, then worry tapped on her mind. The boys had never been so disruptive to customers before, and she hoped it wasn't because her brother was away that they were playing up. Once she finished the order she was working on, Lexi went to the other side of the café. Curious to hear what they were talking about and what was causing her customers to leave, she turned her back to them and made herself busy. The deep tone of their voices were hard to focus on in amongst the noise of the Center, but from bits and pieces she picked up, she was sure they were speaking of a woman. A little disturbed about the innuenco she picked up and the constant bursts of laughter that erupted from them, her brother's words flashed through her mind — *I don't want to hear my sister's name bantered about on the work site.* The counter bell chimed, and she saw Michelle cross the floor to serve an elderly lady. Heart racing, Lexi returned her focus to preparing fresh focaccias, and her ears tuned in to the boy's conversation behind her. Noticing a new voice amongst them, she intensified her focus. The voice was deep and muffled against the din surrounding her, but the inflection was different. Pausing her task, she focused on them, shutting out all other noises, but they all spoke at once.

"So the weekend aye, went well by the looks of that grin."

"It's written all over his face."

"He doesn't have to say anything," another chimed in, his voice followed by raucous laughter.

"Just laying the groundwork, fellas," the presumptive fellow retorted.

"Don't tell us that red-haired fox is putting up a fight?"

"She wouldn't win if she did!" the boastful man responded, relishing his comrade's amusement. "It'll be a challenge, but you know me." More appreciative chuckles sounded. "Hey Lex, can you give me a hand?"

Lexi jumped, dropping the butter knife she held. As it clattered to the floor, she turned to see who spoke to her. It was Michelle. There was a concerned look on her face.

"You ok, boss?" Michelle asked.

Lexi's heart was racing. "Ah, do me a favor first, please. Can you glance at that table of boys and tell me if Brad is amongst them?"

Michelle flicked a glance behind Lexi then nodded her head once. "Yeah, he's there. You sure you ok? Do you want to take your break? Go and spend some time with him?"

The thought repulsed Lexi, and she felt herself gag. Hot tears began to prick her eyes, and she bit down on her lip hard. She was a professional, and she wouldn't run out on her colleague. And furthermore, she would talk to Brad later about what she'd heard. "No, I don't need a break, Michelle. I'm ok. What did you need a hand with?"

The problematic customer took Lexi's mind off what she had overheard and helped her refocus on the job. However, the dirty feeling of being talked about in such a personal way remained. How could Brad be so shameless about her while she was within earshot? Then Lexi remembered that she was filling in for Tiffany this morning. Normally she started at 2:00 p.m. on Mondays. Brad wouldn't have known that Lexi was working. She paused. What if every Monday morning tea consisted of them gathering around to discuss their weekend conquests? Was her brother right about this too? Was she being played? Lexi shuddered at the thought. If the day were running like a normal Monday, then Brad would be dropping in around 3:00 p.m. - afternoon smoko time. She'd deal with him then.

* * * *

Still chuckling at the last customer's witty quip, Lexi pulled the tea cloth off her shoulder and began wiping down the bench. The sun-filled food court wrapped her in warmth that made her heart swell, along with the thought that the evening's Leadership Team meeting drew closer with each passing hour. Smiling as she worked, Lexi tried to organize her thoughts about a game idea that she wanted to talk to Dave about. While the new confidence she was feeling held, she wanted to use it and maybe try to grow it!

A wolf whistle nearby cut into her thoughts, and turning to the direction it came from, she saw Brad making his way toward her. His approach felt like a cloud shadowing her cheerful mood, and she watched as he alighted a seat at the bench and dropped his work bag beside him. Lexi smiled at him as he turned his attention towards her, and she wondered how to bring up the conversation she'd heard earlier. The day had been so busy, she'd not had time to give it much thought. When he didn't say anything to her, her curiosity was roused. Flipping the tea cloth over her shoulder, she crossed her arms and rested a hip against the counter. A lopsided grin appeared on his face as he looked at her. "So, how's my girl's day going?"

"It's fine. How's yours?" Lexi asked. Aware her tone was uncharacteristically cool, she cleared her throat. Not meaning to make known her irritation at him, Lexi smiled. "How're those apprentices treating you?"

"They're alright." He looked at the menu board behind her and pulled out his wallet. "A young pack of pups will always test you out."

Lexi nodded. "Are they who you were talking with at morning smoko?"

His brow furrowed as he looked back at her; his eyes darted to the right as he lifted a shoulder. "Yeah. Why?"

Taking the tea cloth off her shoulder again, Lexi continued wiping down the counters, "Oh, just because I overheard your conversation." While her voice came out melodic, her heart pounded, and she worked a stain on the counter to mask her racing pulse. Her peripheral caught him rise from his seat, and she glanced at him. His expression was dark, and she knew he'd figured it out. Ignoring the stain, she turned to face him.

"So what, you overheard a conversation. What's your point?"

Lexi's eyes narrowed as the memory of him shouting at her on their way to Nick's surprise party flashed to mind. Aware that his irritation would be more audible if they weren't in a public place, Lexi ignored the warning prickling her nerve endings and challenged him. "My point? Are you going to pretend you don't know what part of the conversation I'm referring to?"

Brad's Adam's apple bobbed and a muscle clenched in his jaw; his voice like distant rolling thunder as he flipped a dismissive hand at her. "This is ridiculous, forget the drink." Shaking his head, he picked his bag up and moved to leave.

Lexi stepped forward, wishing he'd not walk away from their unfinished conversation.

Returning, Brad approached the counter with long strides and upon reaching it, thumped a fist on its marble surface. "I can't believe you," he hissed, leaning over the counter. "You're judging me on a conversation you overheard! Did you ever think to ask me what we were talking about before just deciding on your own? Or is ok for you to have little private conversations and not me?"

Her eyes narrowed. "I beg your pardon?"

"Oh, so are you going to pretend that you don't know what I'm referring to?"

Dumbfounded, Lexi shook her head in disbelief. What was he talking about? With a quick glance away to buy thinking time, she scanned the food court, hoping nobody was nearby. When she looked back, it was just in time to see Brad backhand display cups and condiments off the countertop. A mess began pooling at her feet while her lungs burned from lack of breath. Lexi inhaled sharply, raising her eyes to Brad.

He shook his head once more as he stepped back from her. "Don't know why I'm even wasting my time with you."

Lexi felt her jaw drop open as she watched Brad disappear from sight down the escalators. Her breath rushed out the moment his shape was swallowed up by the floor, and her knees weakened. Lexi reached for the bench and leaned against the counter. Her hands were shaking. After taking a moment to breathe, Lexi bowed her head to gather her thoughts; did that just happen? She'd think about that later. Right now she needed to clean the mess Brad made before any clients arrived at the café. Turning to collect the bottles off the floor she spotted Brad coming back up the escalators.

"One iced tea thanks, Lexi."

Lexi spun around at the familiar voice and found Trent settling himself at the counter. His countenance morphed from casual to intense concern as he looked back at her. Lexi swept the fringe from her eyes and smiled before casting a quick glance over her shoulder. Brad was descending the escalators once more. Pulse racing, she turned back to Trent.

He was eyeing the mess on the floor behind her. "Everything ok here, Lex? You look on edge, and there is one big mess on the floor there."

She moistened her lips and took a long deep breath to slow her racing mind. Lexi hadn't told Brad what she'd overheard, but he'd reacted as if she did. And, what was this about private conversations? With a heavy sigh, she waved an indifferent hand to Trent's query. Lexi knew he would sense otherwise, but wouldn't push the topic if she didn't want to speak about it. She smiled and lifted a shoulder. "Yeah, I'm great! Just made a little mess while cleaning the counters. What brings you by? Aren't you meant to be at work?"

Listening to Trent explain how he finished work early and felt impressed to call in on his way home, Lexi wrung out a cloth and began cleaning the mess up on the floor. She knew it was God's prompting that brought Trent to the café on his way home, so that left one question: Why?

TWENTY-TWO

hankful the day was over, Lexi closed up the café and headed out of the Shopping Centre heavy-hearted. After Trent left, she was positive Brad would show up again or be waiting for her in the car park. But to her surprise, he never materialized. After a quick stop at home to change her clothes, Lexi was soon back on the road headed to Dave's place for their Monday night Leadership Team meeting. Just the thought of discussing the Friday night program reignited the flicker of confidence she'd felt over the weekend, and she couldn't wait to get down to business.

Pulling into Dave's driveway, she saw Trent and Hope had already arrived. With a quick glance at her watch, she saw she was early as usual, but what was unusual was Hope being early. After pulling up next to Hope's yellow VW, Lexi shouldered her bag and stepped down from her seat as a roar in the distance closed in. A bright light appeared at the top of Dave's driveway piercing the dark night, and she shaded her eyes. Once Dylan had parked his bike, she turned to him with a grin and waited until he'd kicked out the foot stand before approaching. He took the helmet off, ruffled his hair and winked at her before sitting the helmet on the handlebars. "So, how's the lady of the hour?" Lexi rolled her eyes. "Ha! I'm fine. You?"

He pulled his gloves off, then alighted from the bike and unzipped his jacket. "I'm good." When he paused and looked past her,

Lexi followed his line of vision as he spoke: "Is that Hope's car?"

Lexi nodded, laughing again. "I know! I thought the same thing. Come on you, hurry up."

The door opened as they approached, and Dave welcomed them warmly. Taking a seat next to Hope in the library, Lexi opened her bag. While pulling out her notepad and pen, she asked Hope why she was early.

Hope shrugged, "Mum and Dad were arguing again, so no need for me to hang around."

"Yeah, I hate it when my folks argue too," Lexi said, giving Hope a quick pat on her arm. She was about to ask what they were fighting about when Dave shut the library door and moved to his desk.

"Ok, welcome guys. Glad to see you are all early! Does that mean you're all keen for Friday night?" Lexi nodded, excitement bursting within her, and she caught Dave smile at her. "But before we begin, may I just say, on behalf of all of our church family, Lexi, well done on Saturday night! Not only did the fundraiser blow the predicted revenue out the window, but the artists have contacted me since to offer their support next year! Our webpage is full of feedback, and not one bit of it is negative. Well done."

Sure her face had taken on a shade similar to beetroot, Lexi toyed with her watch as her friends echoed Dave's praise and swapped stories from the night. When the stories slowed, and laughter quieted, Lexi looked around the room. "Thanks, guys. It was all very surreal to me, and I could not have done it without all of your prayers, support, and help. So all praise cannot go to me."

"Sweetie, none of us had to battle anxieties to do what we did. So don't go cheapening what God did for you, and, maybe even *through* you."

Smiling at Hope while those around her agreed, Lexi felt herself blush again. "Ok. I promise I won't. I am very moved and humbled by what took place, but can we move on now?"

The rest of the evening went by in a blur as they organized the Friday night program. Head down, Lexi concentrated on the meeting, taking notes and enjoying the feeling of excitement fluttering within her. Eager for the night to be upon them, she prayed the week would go by fast!

*   *   *   *

"So, Lex, how are you feeling about your first leadership round this week?" Dylan said, taking a sip of his drink as they talked over the meeting afterward at the Beach-Side Hotel. "How's that sitting with you?"

Lexi swirled the contents of her drink as a grin played upon her lips. "I think I'll be fine." She took a sip of her drink. The conversation she'd overheard in the café earlier that day suddenly flooded her mind, and Lexi shuddered as the grimy sensation she'd felt washed over her again. She needed to get it off her chest. "Hey guys, I need to talk to you all about something. It's not meeting related, but I need your advice." Trent sat up in his seat as Hope laid a hand on her arm. Turning to Hope, Lexi found her friend smiling back at her.

"Spill honey," Hope said.

Doing her best to recount the situation without letting the lump forming in her throat become known, Lexi explained how she was feeling. She requested their opinions to help make sense of it all.

"I knew you were hiding something," Trent said, as he leaned back in his seat and crossed his arms. Lexi looked over at Dylan and Hope. Dylan's jaw was locked, and Hope was looking confused.

"Maybe he wasn't talking about you?" she offered.

"No, he was," Dylan said, his voice like steel. "Get rid of him."

Unaccustomed to the serious side of Dylan, Lexi watched as a heated discussion broke out between Hope and her protector. Hope's efforts to defend Brad were met by Dylan's uncompromising position of respect. When Hope tried to offer alternate explanations for Brad's comments, Dylan dismissed her suggestions with a shake of his head as he threw back the rest of his drink. "Alright guys," Trent said, his hands held up between Hope and Dylan. "Look, I'm sorry Lexi, but I have to agree with Dylan. You can ask Brad about it in private. But, I think we all know he'll just cover his tracks. If he's got an agenda regarding you, he'll want to see it through. So my advice? End it, and end it soon."

The lump reappeared in Lexi's throat, and she swallowed past it as she reached for her drink. "I had a feeling you boys were going to say that." She rolled the contents in her glass around, staring into the mocha colored liquid - her thoughts a blurred mix on what had been said and what her conscience was telling her. They were all telling her the same thing, but her heart said otherwise. She wanted to believe the best about people, and Brad certainly had shown her a good side. Besides, didn't everyone have a bad side?

Aware that Dylan and Hope had started up the discussion again, Lexi sighed loudly and wished she hadn't brought the subject up. She placed a hand on Hope's arm silencing her as she looked at the boys, "Guys, that's enough. I will talk to him about it. Thank you for your opinions. My immediate reaction was to end it, but I think I'll talk to him first."

When staff began lifting chairs onto tables, and the sound of vacuum cleaners began humming, Lexi rose, collected her bag off the floor, and shouldered it. "Think I'm going to head off, guys. I'll let you know how it goes with Brad." After saying goodbye, she excused herself from the table. But a hand hooked her elbow. Confused, she looked back at Trent as he released her arm, and she waited as he seemed to pick his words.

"Just remember Lex, your first reaction is most often the right one. Be careful."

TWENTY-THREE

"*D*on't...you...DARE!" Lexi's voice was high pitched and just audible through her laughter as she turned her back to Trent. In an effort to be extra organized for the youth program she was leading out on, Lexi had turned up at Youth with wash baskets already full of water balloons she wanted to use in the icebreaker. However, in hindsight, Lexi knew that was asking for trouble. In no time, the boys had pounced declaring war, and she and Hope had deserted the game props – fast. Now outrun, Lexi found herself at Trent's mercy while somewhere on the church grounds, she heard Hope's squeal and Dylan's echoing laugh. She shook with adrenaline and exertion as she peered over her shoulder at Trent. "I mean it Trent, put it down!"

His mouth turned up in a lopsided grin as he tossed the balloon casually between his hands. "Lost your falsetto, huh?"

"Don't you throw that. I can't be wet before the game starts." Lexi negotiated. Seconds ticked by while she attempted to stare him down.

Trent lowered his arm, and he chuckled. "Ok, I won't throw it."

Lexi narrowed her eyes as she turned to face him. "Truce?"

He grinned, and she opened her palm, not trusting him until she had possession of the water balloon. When the balloon pressed into her palm she lifted her chin at him with a smile and satisfied, she began to turn away.

". . . yet."

She halted and turned back to him, "What did you say?"

Hands in his jean pockets, Trent nudged her with his shoulder back in the direction they were headed. "Me? Nothing at all. So tell me, are you ready for tonight?"

Lexi smirked at him, knowing he was avoiding her question and nodded. "Um, yeah. I'm not nervous at all!" Looking around at the clear afternoon sky, she sighed. It was uncharacteristically warm for early spring, and she couldn't help thinking that God had a hand in it all. Everything was going to go well, she knew it.

"Hey, before I forget," Trent said, as they walked back to the play area. "Nick's finished at the Academy as of 6:00 p.m. tonight, and he wants to see the Tigers play in the Semis over the weekend. Are you free, or do you have plans?"

Lexi picked up the hesitation in his voice and shook her head. She knew he'd be curious to hear if she'd taken his advice about Brad. While she considered how to answer him, excited thoughts filled her mind about Nick coming home. "No, I'm free all weekend. This is great, I can't wait to see him again! Three months have gone so fast though hasn't it?"

Trent paused and looked at her, his green eyes looking right through her. "It sure has. So tell me, what's happening with your other half?"

Cars pulling into the car park drew her attention. Thankful for the interruption, she glanced back at Trent. "Nothing, yet. _

haven't spoken to him." As youth spilled onto the lawn, Lexi put thoughts of Brad aside. Tonight was about the youth, and she set about welcoming them to the night they had planned.

Once everyone's attention was focused her direction, Lexi scooped up a water balloon and indicated the walking plank set up nearby. "Ok everyone, the ice breaker for the evening is called 'Walk the Plank.' When you arrived, everyone was given a number that corresponds to a flag pinned up along the plank. Find your flag. And when your turn comes to walk the plank, you will be dodging these." Gasps of excitement echoed around the grounds as Lexi dropped the water balloon back into the basket, and asked for two teams to form behind Hope and Trent.

Moments later, at her signal, the game erupted into life. Lexi stepped back as high pitched laughter and squeals filled the air. She watched the game unfold, unable to keep the smile from her face. The dedicated youth searched out their flags amongst the chaos, and brilliant smiles showcased their enjoyment of the game. A scrum to her left drew Lexi's attention as a group of mischevious youth trying to drag Dylan towards the plank. She laughed as she heard them encourage each other while they attempted to push him through the gauntlet – their fits of laughter a delight. As they slipped and slid on exhausted water balloon skins, Lexi watched as Dylan humored them and he relented to their wishes. Under relentless bombardment, he stumbled the length of the plank, grabbed his flag then leaped off the end. Then Dylan scooped up a hand full of balloons himself, which sent the youth scattering across the lawn.

"Lexi, this game is awesome!" Hope breathlessly said as she appeared at her side. Hope rarely looked anything other than immaculate, so to see her looking like a drowned rat made Lexi laugh until her stomach hurt.

"How did you get so wet?" Lexi asked in-between breaths. "Have trouble finding your flag?"

"No! Didn't you see Dylan and Trent pelt me behind the play?"

Smiling, Lexi shook her head and turned her attention back to the game. All flags had been collected, and now a fight with the remainder of the water balloons was in play. As the youth filled the twilight atmosphere with their happy laughter, Lexi watched on happily; God was good.

"Hey," Hope elbowed her, breaking her reverie. "How're things with Bradley?"

Irritation pricked Lexi. But, she hid it as she turned to Hope to answer. Then an unexpected impact on her chest knocked the wind from her lungs. With a gasp, she stumbled back as icy water soaked her shirt and trickled down her body. Laughter rang out, and she looked up as Dylan slapped Trent on the back.

"Never said I wasn't going to throw it!" Trent called out to her.

Dylan turned to address the youth while thumbing a gesture over his shoulder. "Hey guys, Lexi's still dry!"

Eyes widening, she watched as Youth from all angles raced toward her with a war-like cry – each and every one armed with water balloons! They weren't serious!

"You better run, sweetie," Hope said, stepping back from her while ringing out her hair.

Lexi turned to flee but had taken no more than a few steps in the opposite direction, when she felt a pair of strong arms enfold her. In an instant, she was tackled to the ground. She managed to wiggle her arms free under the weight holding her and flipped herself over as the first of many water balloons exploded on her body. She shut her eyes as the icy water soaked through her clothes. Any weak pleas she made for mercy came out as laughter, coughs, and splutters, burning her lungs and cramping her stomach. When the bombardment slowed, Lexi opened her eyes. She pushed feebly at Dylan. An exhausted pink balloon clung to the side of his face, which drew the last of her energy out in silent laughter.

When his grip loosened and she felt his weight shift from her, Lexi took a few deep breaths to compose herself. Then she took the hand he offered to help her up. Once on her feet, Lexi looked herself over – not a dry inch anywhere. Lexi playfully shoved Dylan and laughed as he jogged away. Lexi pulled herself together, squared her shoulders, and smoothed her hair. "Alright, everyone! Go dry off. The lesson will be in ten minutes, followed by supper and youth café. See you in the hall in ten."

As Trent and Dylan shepherded the youth towards the hall, Lexi found herself distracted by how the white shirt clung to Dylan's back - a tantalizing sight that highlighted his broad shoulders, narrow waist, and sculpted arms. How had he escaped her notice?

"Earth to Lexi?"

A blush flooded her face, and she turned to Hope. "What?" Hope's smile said it all! Bending down, Lexi picked up a handful of balloon pieces and tossed them at her.

Hope gleefully reciprocated.

Lost in the skirmish that followed, Lexi laughed until tears blurred her eyes. Awareness slowly dawned when a figure approached, and Lexi called for a truce with Hope.

"Babe, can we have a chat for a sec?"

She squinted at the figure in the dim light, "Brad?"

His voice was rough, and his posture seemed rigid. "Yeah."

Signaling for Hope to give them a moment, she approached him as Hope speared off towards the hall. "Of course, sorry I didn't see you there! It's been a crazy evening here. What's up?" Lexi asked between breaths.

He turned and watched Hope depart. Once she disappeared from sight, Brad cleared his throat. "So we go out on Saturday night and have a great time. I see you all awkward on Monday, and you haven't returned my calls all week. I show up here to see you and find you flirting with pretty boy again." His expression was still disinterested; however, the blackness in his eyes held a warning her body reacted to. Aware her heart was starting to thump, she tried to appear casual as she shifted her body away from his. "What do you mean, *again*? There has to be a first in order to be a . . ."

Brad stepped closer. "Don't play stupid. It's embarrassing enough to watch."

Lexi straightened. Her eyebrows raised as she looked back at him. Her mind demanded she put together a coherent sentence instead of the wild haphazard thoughts whirling around at his accusation. Faltering, she declared, "Embarrassed? Try being the topic of an inappropriate conversation by a vulgar pack of males, *then* you'll know about embarrassment!" Lexi stepped past him and swallowed the bile rising in her throat. How dare he crash her night, draw attention to his mood then accuse her of . . .

When Brad spun her around, Lexi tilted off balance but caught herself before landing on the wet ground. The angry man glared at her and barely controlled his demeanor after he released her arm. Lexi rubbed the mark his hand left on her arm as prayers for rescue came to mind.

"Don't you dare walk away from me Lexi! I came here well natured, and so far you've treated me like dirt. I thought you were a better chick than this."

Insulted, she stared at him. Watching his eyes for any flicker of recognition, she spoke; her voice steady, "Brad. I heard you speaking with the boys in the food court on Monday. I had an early shift that day, and you boys were so loud that you could have been heard in the street!" His eyes remained unblinking though is Adam's apple bobbed. Her name was called from the hall, and Lexi stepped back, unwilling to turn her back to him again. "Perhaps you can put it together why I haven't returned your calls this week."

As her name was called out again, Lexi flicked a glance over her shoulder and saw Hope silhouetted in the doorway to the hall. With Hope watching on, Lexi felt safer. So, she squared her shoulders and turned toward the church without looking back.

TWENTY-FOUR

Red and white colored flags danced and fluttered in the breeze high above the forest green turf of The Valley Football Ground. Like a people sending their warriors off to war, the Tigers colors were everywhere. Banners waved. Mascots jested. Voices sang. Movement was down to a shuffle as throngs of people spilled through the gates and filled the stands and boundary line seats. Lexi sat beside Hope along the boundary line and watched the seniors go through their warm-up drills. The sun was warm on her back, the cappuccino in hand was like drinking silk, and there wasn't a worry in her mind. And, she would get to see Nick again today - when he'd finally arrive! It was a perfect morning.

The crowd surrounding the oval was growing by the minute, and Lexi found herself wondering where all the people came from. Never had she seen so many at a semifinal game in the whole time she'd come to watch Dylan play. Maybe it was because the Tigers were coming off a five-year losing streak, and these people were dusting off their memberships? Or, maybe the visiting team had more supporters? Either way, it was great to see the ground full for a change!

"Hey, did you hear Dylan could be up for captaincy next year?" Lexi asked Hope as she watched the captains flip the coin in the middle of the oval.

"No, I hadn't heard that," Hope answered. "But, he'll have to earn it with Josh Anderson nipping at his heels." Lexi looked at Hope and grinned. When Hope turned to look back at her, Lexi brightened her smile and received an elbow in the ribs.

"Right girls, move over," Nick called out moments before he stepped in-between them.

Lexi quickly gathered up her bag and cappuccino and scooted over before Nick ended up on her lap "Hello to you too Nick," Lexi laughed

Nick settled himself on the seat and took a large bite out of the pie he'd purchased. He grinned back at her, savoring the mouthful.

"Lexi," Trent said, taking a seat next to her. "I meant to ask you, how'd it go with Brad Friday night? I didn't see him come in after the water balloon fight."

Uncomfortably, Lexi flicked Trent an uneasy smile. "Well, when I called him on what he'd done, he didn't deny it. And after that, I joined the rest of you inside. Haven't spoken to him since."

"What he do?" Nick asked around a mouthful of pie. Before she could answer, Hope gave Nick a quick summary of what had happened. Nick's expression turned incredulous, and Lexi saw him swallow the mouthful of pie he was working on. "Are you serious? What kind of bloke is he?"

Holding her hands up, Lexi acknowledged Nick's comments – she understood his annoyance. She explained that she couldn't decide what to do until she'd had a proper conversation with Brad about it, and then Lexi requested that the topic be dropped.

With a playful rap on Nick's leg, she added, "You've only just got back, so I'm sure you don't want to hear about my drama. Tell us about the Academy!"

The afternoon seemed to pass in a flash while the fast-paced game played out before them, and Nick shared stories about Academy life. It was clear as Lexi listened to him speak, that Nick had found his niche in life and he excelled at it. His eyes were bright and his smiled beamed. Occasionally she'd meet Hope's eye, and they would share eye rolls and head shakes at some of Nick's stories. As the day moved along, Lexi wished she'd found her niche like Nick. She knew she wanted to work with Youth, but in what context? The field was so broad.

The halftime siren rang out, and Lexi stretched her arms over her head as she yawned and stood to shake out her legs. The oval before her was filling with spectators enjoying their own small games of football, while the fast food vans nearby became over-crowded in the blink of an eye. Thankful they'd brought their own food for the afternoon, Lexi and Hope arranged lunch while Nicks' stories continued. When he spoke about the self-defense course all new recruits had completed, Lexi found her interest heightened. As he described some quick release maneuvers, Lexi found herself fascinated. When Nick asked for a volunteer, she jumped in first.

As the Third Quarter started, and they settled back into their seats, Lexi considered asking Nick to host a self-defense course for the Youth on a Friday night. Making a quick note in her phone to follow up on the idea, she turned her attention back to the game.

The rest of the afternoon passed by at pace as the visiting team clawed their way back in front by Three-Quarter time, then in the Fourth Quarter, the Tigers lifted again and sent their opponents home with a thirty-six-point loss. The grounds echoed with the Tigers anthem, played at a deafening pitch. Spectators were on their feet in riotous celebration, and the players shock hands as they made their way from the ground.

"Tonight's going to be a big one guys," Trent said above the din, clapping along with the anthem. Lexi nodded. Her stomach already in knots with excitement when she exchanged a look with Hope. Party time!

*　*　*　*

Shoes swinging loosely from her hands, Lexi laughed as Hope tried in vain to defend herself. The night was clear, and the stars shone with brilliance above them as they walked the quiet nature strip leading to Lexi's home. Having run short of cash, their taxi driver had dropped them five blocks from her home and the man wasn't willing to negotiate an extended fare. Lexi turned her face to the evening breeze and breathed deeply of the fresh springtime air, fragrant with the scent of jasmine and rose. She smiled. At least it was a beautiful night for a walk. Beside her, Hope continued her cause, and Lexi elbowed her off the footpath. "Oh, Hope, you did so throw yourself at Josh. You didn't trip, you didn't *not* see him, and you didn't leave your phone on the bar." Hope fell silent, but Lexi could see her grinning in the street lamp light and sighed happily. "It was a great night, wasn't it?" Lexi asked.

"The best!" Hope said, her eyes closed in rapture as she meandered the footpath, "I can't wait for the Vote Count night next week. Has Dylan given you the tickets yet?"

Glancing at a passing car, Lexi nodded. "He's given me two, one for Brad and I. But I haven't decided yet if I'm going to bring him. Just too many things aren't adding up. And while I want to give him the benefit of the doubt, sometimes I . . . " trailing off her sentence as her phone vibrated, Lexi fished in her bag for it.

Baby, it's 1:20 in the morning, and I cannot stop thinking about you. Can I come and see you in the morning? I need to talk to you. I hope this doesn't wake you up. Brad xx

Staring at the text message, Lexi felt conflicted. Brad was sweet and thoughtful, but was it a game? Her brother certainly thought so, and he'd always looked out for her. Was the look of hurt in Brad's eyes last night at Youth group really what he was feeling, or was he pretending to be hurt to get under her skin and make her feel bad? She'd heard of guys playing games like that before.

Sighing again, Lexi looked at Hope. "Sorry, what did you say?"

"I asked what the rest of your sentence was, you kind of stopped talking as you opened your phone. Was the message from Brad?"

Nodding her head, Lexi sighed again and turned up her driveway while pulling the house key from her bag. "Nothing gets past you."

"Or past you!" Hope countered with a giggle. "And for your information, I actually *didn't* know Josh had gone to get some fresh air when I went outside. That was a coincidence."

Glancing at Hope, Lexi rolled her eyes. "Sure it was."

TWENTY-FIVE

Waking with a start, Lexi pushed herself up. She looked around her room; her mind in a daze. When her eyes fell upon Hope asleep on the blow-up mattress by the window, the night before came flooding back, as well as Brad's message. Running a hand over her hair, Lexi reached for the phone. No more messages from Brad illuminated her screen, so Lexi opened the last one he sent and re-read it. She had nothing planned for the day, and her parents and Shaun were home. So, if Brad wanted to come and speak with her, Lexi would be safe. Frowning, she wondered why her safety came to mind. With a shrug, Lexi dismissed the thought and pushed back the covers. Lexi exited the room quietly and padded to the bathroom to shower and get ready for the day. She returned to her bedroom to find Hope ending a phone call.

"Sorry to up and run, Lex, but work needs me."

Lexi giggled as Hope continued to sit on the mattress with a look of disinterest on her face, clearly stalling.

"Would you like to join us for breakfast?" Lexi offered.

Hope shook her head and pushed herself up with a grunt. "Nar, I better get moving."

"Ok, well the bathroom is free if you'd like to freshen up. I'll catch you downstairs before you leave." The smell of French toast and roasting coffee beans greeted her as she approached the living area. Lexi inhaled deeply as she entered the room and found her family gathered around the breakfast table.

"How was last night?" Shaun asked as she joined them, scraping the last of the scrambled eggs off of his plate.

Lexi poured herself a coffee, surprised he asked. She chuckled as memories flooded her mind. "It was fantastic. We were at the club-rooms celebrating until well after midnight."

Shaun nodded as he collected his plate and cutlery. "That's great. Hope the Tigers win the cup." His chair scraped as he pushed back from the table before heading to the kitchen.

Reaching for the French toast, Lexi ate her breakfast in silence as her parents read the Sunday newspapers. Shaun's abruptness unsettled Lexi. They used to be close, but her relationship with Brad had strained that closeness. When Shaun walked from the room without further conversation, he confirmed it. After finishing her breakfast and seeing Hope off, she decided she would take Brad up on his request to see her. By sunset at least one of the relationships in her life would be righted.

* * * *

The patio sliding doors opened, and Lexi looked up from her book. Brad approached her like a puppy caught ripping up cushions - a bouquet of flowers peeking out from behind his back. When he pulled a chair out adjacent to her and laid the small bouquet of tulips on the table, she noted they were her favorite flower. Had she told him that?

"These are for you."

Lexi flicked her eyes up to him at his soft-spoken words, but she kept her expression guarded - not wanting him to relax yet.

With a tilt to her head, she questioned, "Why?"

His head dropped, and Lexi watched Brad clench his hands together on his lap. Was he blushing? She squinted at him.

After a moment he sniffed, and with a wry grin looked back at her. "You're not going to make this easy on me, huh?"

She closed her book and put it on the table, then crossed her arms. "Well, no." His countenance dropped, and she felt her breath catch. Doubt suddenly crossed her mind. What if Brad decided she wasn't worth the effort?! Lexi's confidence slipped, and she reached for the flowers. "Thank you for these though."

He caught her hand before she took hold of the flowers, and surprised, she watched as he cradled it in his own. Uncertainty flickered in her mind, and when he looked up at her, she was struck by the tenderness in his features.

"Listen." His voice was rough. The thumb that stroked the back of her hand chipped away at the pieces of Lexi's defensive barriers.

Determined to hold onto her common sense, Lexi listened as Brad explained the context of the conversation she overheard. Against her will, Lexi's pique softened as he spoke and she suddenly understood how he saw things. Lexi moved uncomfortably, tangled up between what her heart and mind where telling her.

Brad pulled his chair closer, and Lexi closed her eyes as he stroked her cheek, his voice a light breath upon her face. "Lexi, I hate how I hurt you, and I hate how a stupid, immature conversation between the idiots I work with, may have cost me the best thing that's ever happened to me."

Lexi opened her eyes, took a deep breath, and shook her head. Something still nibbled at her conscious. "Brad," she said, wishing her confidence would return, and her voice would steady. "How can I believe you?" Lexi asked as she watched him closely. "You sound genuine, but too many things aren't adding up." She searched his face and asked again, "How can I believe this is true?"

Brad pulled his chair closer still, and her stomach tightened at the brush of his thighs on either side of her own. Lexi's pulse began to gallop as he leaned forward on the armrests of her chair. Cordoned, she caught her breath.

"Ask me anything you want to know, anything."

There was just one question that troubled her conscious and needed an answer. With a shaky breath, Lexi summoned her voice. "How did you g . . . get my phone n . . . number?"

Brad's eyes flickered, and he dropped his head. She heard his soft chuckle and felt a frown tickle her brow as she waited for the answer. His head came back up, and the lopsided grin he wore warmed her body, his full mouth tempting in its nearness. "I knew this question would come up. Ok, when I told you I got it off Shaun, I was telling the truth . . . only, *he* wasn't aware he gave me the number."

"What?" Lexi breathed, a mix of curiosity and misgiving fighting it out in her mind.

"Well, I knew Shaun wouldn't give me your number if I asked for it; so, I went through his phone while he left it unattended one day."

Open mouthed, Lexi stared at him. Brad leaned back, holding his hands up. "I know that was dodgy, but I just wanted to see you and surprise you."

Lexi pushed her chair back and rose, putting the table between them.

Brad stood and moved towards her, "Look I know what you're most likely thinking, but I promised you the truth so that you'd trust me again. I can't take back what I did, but I don't regret it for a moment."

Lexi covered her mouth and turned her back to him. Flattered he'd go to such lengths to get her number, she worried about what kind of person would do that in the first place. His hand fell gently upon her shoulder, and she turned at the slight pressure. Gazing back at him, Lexi discovered the waiting . . . the hoping in his eyes. And without a doubt, she knew Brad was trying. He gave her the truth when she asked for it. The racing pulse visible in his throat added to her confirmation. Confidence returning, she decided to give him the benefit of the doubt one more time and nodded her head, "Ok, I believe you."

Scooped up in his arms before she could finish her sentence, Lexi allowed a smile to light her features as Brad nestled his face into her hair. Then, put back on her feet, she chuckled at the smile on his face as he stepped back. "Tell you what, my housemate is out this evening. Why don't you come over, and I'll cook you tea?"

Tilting her head, Lexi crossed her arms. "You'll cook?"

He nodded. "Anything you want. Say, 7:30 p.m.?"

She nodded. "7:30 p.m. sounds great."

TWENTY-SIX

*W*ith a last-minute glance in the visor mirror, Lexi reapplied her gloss lip balm and smoothed her hair out. Her stomach was full of butterflies, and taking deep breaths weren't settling them. She felt light as a feather and couldn't wait to see the dinner Brad had prepared for her.

He opened the door as she approached, and the scents that greeted her brought a smile to her face. "Smells amazing." "Let's hope it taste as good," Brad said, greeting her with a kiss.

Lexi filled her lungs with the warming scents of Rosemary and Thyme as she made her way to the living area, where Brad had created an intimate setting with candles and low light. Eyes widening, she looked around the room, impressed by his efforts. Lexi turned to Brad when he entered the room behind her. "Well, I wasn't expecting this." Slow Jazz music filled the space with the click of a button, and while it wasn't her thing, Lexi smiled at

Brad, admiring his efforts. He gestured for her to sit at the table, and as she did, Lexi enquired after his housemate.

"He is out on a date too," Brad said from the kitchen serving window. As she poured a drink of water, Lexi listened to the play-by-play of Brad's afternoon escapades – the exile of his roommate for the evening, his efforts to create a romantic meal, and the case of nerves he fought whenever he thought of it all.

"I'm sure it will be great, Brad," Lexi called out to him. He appeared moments later and laid a platter of sliced meats, roasted vegetables, and gravy on the table. Then he sat heavily in the seat opposite her. A tired grin lit his eyes. "Hook in."

Thanking him again, Lexi filled her plate, then topped up her glass. As they ate, Brad enquired after how the Leadership Team was going, and also how the presentation for Uni was coming along. Surprised the conversation was circling more around her than him, she answered his questions and accepted his praises. Lexi found any effort to steer the conversation back to him re-directed. Embarrassed, she laid her knife and fork on the plate and pushed it back. "Why are you asking me so many questions, I feel like I'm being interviewed or something?"

Brad eyed her over the rim of his glass, and she held his gaze as long as she felt comfortable. Unnerved, Lexi reached for her glass.

"Am I embarrassing you with my interest again?"

Memories from their initial meeting flooded her, and Lexi grinned awkwardly. Brad's interest had always been intense, but she didn't understand why. Maybe there was more to her than she'd ever thought - the kids at youth group certainly thought so! They were always all over her. She put her glass down and looked back at him. Summoning up the confidence she had recently discovered, Lexi held his gaze. "Not as much, but yes, a little."

Brad rose and collected their plates while telling her he had one more surprise. Then he disappeared to the kitchen again. Curious, Lexi watched him. Relaxed, she thanked the Lord silently for helping her bring peace to one of her relationships. Happiness filled Lexi - her earlier wish had come true. She'd misunderstood Brad's conversation, and he'd misinterpreted her friendship with Dylan. She reached for her glass and drained it, amazed at the little things that could cause so much upset.

"Ok, look."

Lexi turned at Brad's announcement and found him entering the room awkwardly, carrying a cupcake stand filled with Red Velvet Cupcakes decorated with cream cheese frosting. Her favorite. He placed it down in the middle of the table and looked at her, a wide grin forming on his face. "Go on. Ask."

Lexi breathed a chuckle as she reached for a cupcake and began peeling off the casing. "How did you know these are my favorite cupcakes?" He winked in reply, returning to his seat. She scooped a dollop of frosting off the cupcake with her finger and raised an eyebrow at him. Brad took a cupcake and bit heartily into it, grinning back at her through the mouthful.

Hope. Only Hope knew her fetish for Red Velvet cupcakes. Brad must have asked her best friend. Finishing the delicious treat, Lexi shrugged. Brad had wiles about him she hadn't even begun to discover yet!

The cupcake was delicious, and after joking that he couldn't possibly have made them, Lexi dusted off her hands and resisted the urge to take a second one. "Brad this has been such a great night, thank you so much. Oh, before I forget, next Saturday is the Football Vote count, and Dylan gave me two tickets for us." Rising, she waited for him to do likewise while fishing his ticket out of her bag. As she handed it to him, she was sure she saw disappointment flicker behind his eyes. She took his hand as they strolled to the door. "If I didn't have a big day planned tomorrow with the presentation for Uni and all, I'd have stayed longer. I had such a great night. Thank you for doing this."

Pulling the front door open, Lexi turned to Brad to give him a kiss goodbye when he laid a hand against the door, closing it.

"So, that's it?"

His smile was charming and voice gentle, but there was a subtle hostility that caused the hairs on the back of her neck to rise.

Unsure, Lexi grinned. "What?"

He brushed the fringe from her eyes as he stepped closer, leaning on the hand pressed against the closed door. "It kind of goes without saying, or do I need to explain it to you?"

A warning zipped up her spine, and Lexi stepped back. The door behind closed off her retreat as Brad's arm encircled her waist.

He drew her into him, and she giggled, masking the unease she felt. "Come on Brad it's late; I need to get going."

His eye's traveled her face as his hand cupped the back of her head, his voice was teasing as he ignored her request. "A man doesn't go to all this effort for a kiss, Lexi."

Pulled into him as his kiss finished the sentence, she found her unease confirmed. Lexi's heart slammed into overdrive, and she pressed her hands against his chest, pushing him back. "Whoa, what are you expecting?!"

"C'mon, you're not that naive." Brad chuckled, and she stiffened.

A mix of panic and anger flooded Lexi as she refused to be pulled into his arms. She glared at him, trying to sum up her thoughts. "Are you saying, you planned this whole evening hoping to get laid at the end of it?"

He smirked. "Well . . . not *hoping*."

Pulled into another passionate embrace, Lexi pushed at him, disgusted at his insistence and the sudden turn of the evening. Breaking off his kiss, she clawed at the arms around her. "Get away from me, Brad! I'm going home!"

Ignoring her protests, Brad moved her from the door and began shuffling Lexi back into his home. Passionately, he bit down on her neck.

Angry tears pricked Lexi's eyes as she struggled against his vice-like hold. When they passed a doorway, Lexi reached out a hand and clutched the frame. "Brad, I'm serious. Let me go, this isn't funny!"

"I'm serious too," he countered, plucking her fingers from the doorway. "I've gone to a lot of effort for you, it's about time you give something to me."

Her fingers gave way under his prying, and without thought of consequence, Lexi stomped at his instep hoping the heels she wore struck their mark. They did.

Brad swore violently; his grip intensifying. An iron-like fist took hold of her hair and jerked Lexi's head back. Eyes glued to the ceiling above her as her breaths shortened, Lexi felt as helpless as a kitten picked up by its scruff.

"Stop it!" Brad snarled, jerking her head again. "I'm sick of playing games with you. Things have never taken this long before, and I'm furious it's come to . . ." His words trailed off as the sound of a door opening and slamming shut echoed through the house.

Did she imagine it?

Thrust away from him as a voice closed in on them, Lexi stumbled backward through a doorway. Landing on his water bed, Lexi struggled to right herself while Brad's attention was focused outside the room. Without any grace, she heaved herself to the edge of the bed. Brad tried to distract whoever was visiting, and Lexi regained her feet as an obviously drunk Gavin appeared in the doorway. Brad's roommate. Dread sat like a weight in her stomach as wild thoughts crashed in her mind.

"Oh well, least your night is going better than mine," Gavin said, slurring his words as his appearance turned bitter. "You're looking pretty Le . . ."

"That's your problem, not mine," Brad said as he pulled Gavin from the doorway and tried to move him down the hall. Then Gavin shoved him back.

As the two men began arguing, Lexi seized the small window of opportunity. Without a second thought, she propelled herself past the boys and raced to the front door without looking back.

TWENTY-SEVEN

The lump in Lexi's throat would not move, but she tried to clear her throat once again as she continued her phone call to Dave. He answered in his cheery voice, and Lexi felt her eyes begin to burn.

"I'm s. . . sorry, Dave. I'm just not feeling well enough to come to the meeting tonight." Her friends shouted encouragement in the background for her to come in, and Lexi bit down hard on her lip. Fearful the catch in her voice would betray her reason for not attending the Leadership Team meeting, Lexi spoke slowly and steadily. However, Dave's voice elicited a heavy desire to be amongst their company. Lexi shut her eyes, as if shutting them all out and ended the call. She hadn't really lied – for the third time that day – she thought as she sat heavily on the edge of her bed, as fresh tears blurred her sight. Her presentation had been scheduled for that morning, and unable to face the University auditorium filled with her peers, she made a tearful plea to reschedule for the following Monday. Her Professor agreed, but only after gruffly stating no further extensions would be granted. Then, after canceling work that afternoon, she'd returned to lay on her bed. Lexi was thankful she had the day to herself to think and pray uninterrupted.

Her phone buzzed into life, breaking the silence in the darkened room, and she jumped. With a glance at the floor where she'd thrown it after Brad's name had appeared on the screen moments ago, Lexi debated her interest in the unknown caller. Curiosity won over, and she crossed the room to read the message. It was from Hope: *"Hey sweets, it's not like you to not come to Leadership Team. So, I'm coming over after we finish here. And, there may be three men in tow. So get dressed. Hope. XX"*

A flicker of a smile played upon Lexi's mouth for the first time that day, and Hope's message gave her the motivation she needed to shower and get dressed. It would be a difficult night ahead, and Lexi hadn't even spoken to her family about what happened yet.

* * * *

Lexi looked up from her book after her mum commented on her whereabouts. She craned her neck and viewed four welcome faces as they crossed the living room toward her. Lexi rose to embrace each of her friends as they stepped out onto the patio, and she became emotional again. Tears slipped in a silent stream down her cheeks as she retook her seat.

Hope was beside her before she could reach for the tissues. "I knew it! I knew something was up," Hope said, her voice full of worry. "What's happened, and what's that on your neck?"

"Are they . . . bite marks?" Nick asked raising an eyebrow.

Unable to meet their eyes, nor speak past the lump in her throat, Lexi zipped up her turtle neck sweater and shrugged. Biting her lip as it began to quiver, she wiped her nose.

"Think I'll go get some tea," Trent said.

At Trent's quiet remark, Lexi looked up, and she watched him retreat toward the kitchen until her eyes blurred over. A hand fell upon her leg, and she wiped her eyes before turning. Hope's eyes were searching in the flickering fairy light around them. With a glance at Dylan and Nick, Lexi saw concern and awkwardness in their expressions too. She took an uneven breath and wondered where to start. Hearing the words in her head and saying them out loud were proving very different things. And, if the boys were uncomfortable with her emotional state already . . .

"Sweetie," Hope said, interrupting her thinking. "Just spit it out. Whatever it is."

Shaking her head, Lexi turned back to her friends and summoned her voice. "I need to end things with Brad." She reached for a tissue as Trent re-entered carrying a tray of mugs and a pot of tea. Hope gasped, and Lexi faced her. "Why?" Hope tentatively asked at the same time Dylan sat forward in his seat.

Staring into her tissue, Lexi felt numb. Her lungs felt tight, and she took a long deep breath. "Well, last night, I think he was going to . . ." trailing off as she felt a wave of emotion hit her, Lexi blew her nose and wiped the tear tracks off her cheeks. "I think he was, um, . . . I think he was going to rape me." Lexi covered her mouth as soon as the words were out, and then she shut her eyes as she sniffed back another sob. She felt her friend's reactions without seeing them. The chair that scraped back all of a sudden would be Dylan standing; the foul word would have come from Nick; the hand gripping her leg was Hope; and, Trent would be in prayer.

"But, he didn't?" Dylan's controlled words spoke volumes in the silence that followed, and Lexi raised her eyes slowly to him. Dylan's expression was unreadable, but a fierceness flashed in his eyes as he looked at Lexi that caused her to tremble. She shook her head once in answer.

"Give me the phone! I'll break-up with the mongrel for you," Nick said.

"Nick, leave it. Lexi needs to do it when she's ready."

Looking at Trent as he addressed Nick, Lexi dried her eyes. He was right, and what better time to do it while her friends were around to offer the support she needed. Pushing her hair back, she nodded. "Hand me my phone." Nick pushed it across the table to her, and she scooped it up, looking at the screen: one missed call and one message from Brad. Ignoring both, she opened his contact. With her finger hovering above the call function, Lexi looked around her friends once more before swiping the screen. Each trill of the call tone stretched her nerves as she waited for him to answer; her limbs were heavy and quivered with anxiety. When the call rang out to his answering machine, Lexi eased her breathing. But she caught the shake of Trent's head as she prepared to leave a message, and she quickly hung up the phone. "What?"

"You can't leave a break-up message. Otherwise, he can claim he never got it. You need to speak with . . ."

The phone rang, and Lexi jumped as Trent fell silent, gesturing to her phone. Looking at the screen, she felt her breath catch seeing Brad's name. With a shaky swipe of her thumb, she answered his call.

"Baby! I'm so happy you called," Brad's voice came down the line. "Listen, about last night . . ."

"It's over, Brad." Lexi fixed her gaze on the patio table tiles and fingered a small chip in one of them to keep herself focused and voice firm, even though she couldn't summon up more than a whisper. His silence lengthened, and her chest tightened. She cleared her throat. "Did you hear me? We are over. I don't want to see you again." Unsure when he didn't respond, Lexi looked up at her friends just as the line went dead. She held the phone out from her head and stared at it, while a cold sensation of fear coiled in her gut. "He hung up."

Nick muttered another foul word as he rose, joining Dylan where he stood away from the table. She looked at Trent, but he had his head bowed, and Hope was quiet beside her.

"Well, what now?" Lexi asked.

Nick turned at her question, his jaw clenched as he crossed his arms. "We hope he's not a textbook case."

TWENTY-EIGHT

"*S*o any word from you know who this week?"

Lexi shook her head and handed Hope a box of items from the back of her car. "No, thank the Lord. I've been freaked out all week though expecting him to call or show up at work." With the last box balanced on her hip, Lexi locked up her Jeep and followed Hope inside the hall. Once she offloaded her box onto the stage, Lexi began unpacking its contents. Hope's sigh prompted Lexi to ask, "You ok?" Hope nodded, but appeared to be a million miles away. Touching her arm lightly, Lexi repeated her question.

"Yeah, I'm ok. Just . . . what happened to you. I mean, Brad was so nice! I can't believe he'd turn like that."

A shudder ran through Lexi at the memory, and she continued unpacking her box - laying out the paper, pens, glue, and cardboard cutouts in neat piles. "Can we not talk about it, Hope? I just want to forget about it." Hope dropped the subject, but even that small reminder ignited Lexi's memories. Clamminess broke out on her palms, and her mouth dried up. Lexi moistened her lips and tried to push past the haunting reminders with a forced smile, "Ok. Is this all we need?"

"Yep, I think so," Hope answered cheerfully, just as Dave entered the hall. He was followed by Nick and Dylan handballing a football between one another. "I hope the youth enjoy this little activity. Bit slower than our usual games, but it should still be a good one."

Lexi tipped her chin towards the boys, attempting confidence she was far from feeling and greeted them with a smile. "I'm sure they'll love whatever it is that Dave has planned," Lexi said.

"Evening, girls," Dave called, waving them over to him. "Let's huddle for a moment." Once reaching the small huddle, Dave informed them that Trent was running late and needed someone to fill in.

The youth minister looked at Lexi, and her stomach dropped.

"Lexi, I know it's not been an easy week for you, and praise God you're here with us. However, I'm wondering how you might feel about swapping your scheduled youth café role with Trent's leading role this week?"

Though she knew that was what he was going to ask, Lexi still felt trapped. If she said no, she'd let the team down. If she said yes, it would be out of obligation not desire. She shifted her weight and opened her mouth to answer no, but the word caught in her throat. All of a sudden, she realized if she said no, she'd be declaring God wasn't big enough to help her. Surprised at her doubt, she chose to put her faith to work instead and dipped her head. "Ok. I'll help out as much as I can. What do I need to do?"

Lexi offered a weak smile at Dave's nod of approval, and she acknowledged the slap on the back that Nick gave her. She listened as Dave described what she missed from the Leadership Team meeting earlier that week. The activity was simple. The youth sat in a large circle, and everyone was given a card with their name on it. Each card was passed to the right as a card from the left was received. They had twenty seconds to think of an encouraging word, phrase, or Bible text to write on the card about the titled person, before passing it on. The activity continued until each participant held their own card once more, and then they could take home a list of positive attributes others saw in them. The game appealed to Lexi, and she felt her spirit lift. Her role was small, and the game fit her style perfectly.

As the group disbanded and each of her friends headed off to do their part in the evening, Lexi took a deep breath and blew it out. Resting her hands on her hips, she wondered what she should do. If she were on café duty – as scheduled – she'd go to the kitchen and begin the setup. Deciding to check the items required for the activity, Lexi walked towards the stage. A voice called to her, and Lexi glanced over her shoulder. Trent jogged toward her, and she smiled, surprised to see him. "What are you doing here?

You were going to be late!"

"Change of plans," he said between breaths, coming to a stop in front of her. "Look, I'm sorry to do that to you. Are you alright to continue, or do you want me too?"

Before she could answer him, the hall doors burst open as half a dozen youth entered. Loud chatter and laughter soon filled the room as more and more arrived. Lexi signaled for Trent to follow her to the kitchen. Once the doors swung closed behind them, she picked up their conversation. "Yeah, I'm fine to cover you tonight. Dave told me about what we're doing for the night, and I should be fine."

Trent nodded, his keen green eyes never straying from her. "You're sure? The youth won't know any different."

She dropped her head. The way out was in front of her; she could shrink back to where she felt comfortable and take the easy part for the night. The team would understand. But she would know, and she had decided to put her faith in action and trust herself to God's care. She wouldn't back out now. "Thanks, Trent," Lexi said, raising her head to look at him. "But I'll do it. I'll be ok."

"Ok, well get out there and start. I'll get the café ready."

Feeling a slap on her back as she headed out the doors, Lexi grinned as she re-entered the hall to find Dave on the stage addressing the gathered audience. She made her way over to Hope and waited with her while Dave explained the activity before handing the night over to them. As Hope and Dylan began organizing the youth in a large circle on the hall floor, Nick appeared by her side and handed her some papers and pens.

"Here hand these out. You take this side; I'll take the other," Nick said.

Once the cards were handed out, Lexi took her seat once more against the side of the hall and watched the youth interact with each other as they filled out the cards. An idea tickled her mind, and she sat up, watching them closely. They were all quiet and focused. On occasion, they glanced around the room before dropping their eyes back to the page before them, sharing silent laughs and gestures. What was it about the activity that intrigued her? Something fit. But what? A body sat down heavily next to her, and she grinned at Nick as he made himself comfortable. Then she returned her attention to the youth, determined to work out why her system was energized.

"What are you so deep in thought about?" Nick asked.

Sighing, Lexi sat back in her seat. "Well, I'm trying to figure out what it is about this activity that has me so intrigued. I mean, I love the idea behind it, and they all seem to love it. They're praising one another, searching for the other's value - it's so encouraging!"

Nick shrugged. "Hopefully they learn something from it."

Crossing her arms, she sniffed. "I wonder if they express whatever they're writing on the cards to each other's face. 'Cos that's really more important." Lexi pushed her soul-searching aside and elbowed Nick when she noticed Dylan and Hope add new cards to the activity. "What's going on here?"

Nick's casual expression remained unaltered as he watched on, though she noticed a grin form as he looked back at her. "Again, no idea."

Mystified, Lexi sat forward and watched her friends. Did they know something she didn't or was it simply a change of plans? Dave was good at those. Catching Dylan's eye as he glanced her way, Lexi knew by his wink that he was "in the know." And, he wasn't about to tell her. She leaned towards Nick, her voice hushed. "Dylan knows."

Nick cleared his throat and rested an ankle over his knee. 'I wondered what he and Dave were whispering about earlier. Must be a slight change in the game plan."

A thrill ran up her spine. Lexi shot Hope a querying glance and received a shrug in response. She began to fidget. Surely Dave wasn't going to throw another change into the evening without telling her. "Doesn't look like Hope knows either. Wonder if Trent knows?" Lexi mused. She needed to know if Dave's sudden switch would put her on the spot! She'd ask Trent what he knew. Rising from her seat, Lexi felt Nick's hand encase her arm and ease her back down next to him.

"Does it matter who knows?" he asked.

A frown darkened her features as she looked back at him. "I just want to know what is happening is all."

Nick's grip eased, and he linked his hands behind his head. "Well, my hunch is you'll find out along with the rest of us. Until then just relax a little."

The unsettled feelings inside agitated Lexi as she tried to appear relaxed. In the meantime, she tried to convince herself that Dave would keep his promise to her. As Dylan and Hope came to sit with them, Lexi watched as Dave collected the extra cards then made his way to the stage. She leaned forward in her seat and kept her eyes on those extra cards that were now tucked under his arm. With her head resting in the palm of her hand, she listened to Dave's message. Lexi felt his short talk to the young people gathered could have been for her. As she continued to listen, the words cut deep, and she lowered her eyes. Talks on remembering your self-worth and listening to your conscious had always captivated and inspired her; however, after Dave's message on the topic, Lexi found herself feeling guilty. Her relationship with Brad had confused everything; how could she have been so wrong about him and conned so easily? Why didn't she go with her gut instinct the moment it started challenging her?

As Trent opened the café, the hall erupted into life with music and ball games. And, Lexi knew she had to go. The desire for quiet retrospection overwhelmed her. With a quick goodbye to her friends, she waved goodbye to Dave and headed towards the exit. "Lex, hold up!"

Hearing Dylan call out after her, she turned slowly and waited by the door for him to catch up. He was holding one of the cards Dave had collected.

"What's up?" she asked as he approached.

"Don't forget this," he said, holding the card out toward her. "See you tomorrow night?"

Taking the card, Lexi nodded. "I'll be there. Wouldn't miss it."

Dylan dipped his head and the smile he wore brightened before he turned and jogged back into the hall.

Once tucked up inside her car, Lexi switched on the interior light - keen to know what was on the card Dylan handed to her. Opening it, her eyes scanned the words on the page moments before tears blurred it from sight.

~ What we love about LEXI ~

Gorgeous Smile

Cute

My Best Friend!

Someone I look up to ☺

Confident

Always Happy

Strong

Kind

Awesome Cook

Always looks great

Smiles a LOT!

Funny

TALL

Makes youth night fun

Helpful

Smart

My role model

So Pretty!

Friendly

Thoughtful

Dazzling eyes xx

TWENTY-NINE

"You ready?" Lexi asked Hope.

With scarcely controlled excitement, Lexi paused before the frosted glass doors of the Valley Stadium's function room and grinned at her friend. Smoke curled from under the doors and a pulsating rhythm could be felt through the floor. Hope was already dancing.

"Yes," Hope said, readjusting her black, strapless dress. "Let's get in there!"

Lexi's eyes adjusted to the smoke haze and the disco lights in the moment before Hope grabbed her arm.

"I'll catch up with you later!" Hope yelled over the music.

Before Lexi could answer, Hope was gone. She caught sight of her friend among the crowd and watched as the confident girl crossed the room towards the bar. A familiar young man turned as Hope approached him. Lexi shook her head. Josh. The amorous glances between her friend and the footballer sparked, and Lexi grinned.

Nervously, Lexi smoothed out the silky crimson material of her tea-length dress and fiddled with the diagonal diamante strap. "I can't believe you've left me for him, Hope," she muttered, averting her eyes from a group of men nearby. Spying Trent and Nick reclined on lounge chairs watching the big screen, Lexi tossed her hair back and began to weave herself through the crowded dance floor toward them. She could enjoy the night without her wingman, she didn't need Hope to . . .

Spun back on herself as an arm encircled her waist, Lexi teetered like a deer on ice until another body ended her desperate attempt to regain her balance. Heat rose up Lexi's neck and pooled in her face. She regained her footing while the strong arms held her. Lexi pulled herself away from the imposing form that held her and opened her mouth to excuse herself. Then she blinked.

"Is that a new dance move?" Dylan asked, eyebrows raised.

"Dylan!" Lexi shouted over the music, surprised to see him on the dance floor. "You almost tripped me up!" He spun her away from him, and she heard him laugh.

"How high are those heels you're wearing?" he asked, drawing her back. "You're almost as tall as I am!"

"Four inches! So, go easy on the spins, buddy!" Lexi laughed as she danced to the DJ's lively mix of electronica and what sounded like Latin. She felt fabulous! Her silken dress swirled around her, and the lights bounced off the diamante detail - drawing attention to her. But this time she didn't mind the attention. Not while she was dancing with Dylan. It was safe, and she smiled brightly at him as he attempted to dip her.

As the DJ changed the music to a slow rhythm, Lexi tossed her hair back and stood with her hands on her hips while she caught her breath. Couples began entwining nearby, and she looked around, a knowing grin spread upon her face. 'Ah, the old fast to slow music change cliché, aye? Wanna get a drink?"

Dylan chuckled, and she looked back at him just as his arm circled the curve of her back and drew her to him. "Well, I guess I shouldn't do this then," he said, a slow smile curved on his face as he took her hand. "Because you'd expect it, right?"

Lexi's eyes widened at Dylan's flirtatious manner, and she allowed him to move her into the slower rhythm, thinking how to counter his comment. A thought flashed to mind, and she laid an arm across the back of his shoulders, "Well then, I guess I shouldn't do *this*," she purred, "because you'd expect it."

Dylan chuckled again, only this time the sound held an intimate note as he broke their gaze. His arm encircled her lower back further.

Their closeness registered, and her smile dropped away as energy ignited. She could feel his cheek against her hair. The scent of Dylan's cologne surrounded her, and for the first time, her mind wandered down a path it'd never gone before.

He cleared his throat, breaking her reverie. "You're stunning tonight, Lex."

Her body warmed at the unusual husky tone of his voice against her ear, and she caught her breath. When Dylan pulled back and looked at her, a tremor ran through her as his eyes traveled her face.

"I almost didn't recognize you when you walked in."

A light frown tickled her brow as she looked back at him. "What's going on?" she asked, her voice betraying her racing heart with its breathy note. But Lexi needed her suspicions confirmed. When Dylan lifted his eyes from her as if in thought, she felt a heaviness weave into her limbs as she waited for his answer - though the way he was holding her spoke louder than any words could.

"What is he doing here?" Dylan said, his tone cold.

Dylan's hold on her stiffened as he stopped the dance. As if waking from a trance, Lexi looked up at him blinking. "Who?"

A muscle worked in Dylan's jaw as his eyes fixed somewhere behind her, and Lexi looked over her shoulder through their embrace. Immediately she felt the fine hair on the back of her neck rise. "I don't know," Lexi said on a caught breath. Just then Dylan's arms fell away from her, and he moved to step around her. "No," she said, a palm against his chest to prevent his intended movement. "I'll deal with him. I have to. Like Trent said." As Lexi turned from Dylan and took a step to move away, she felt Dylan's hand hook her upper arm. Looking back at him, Lexi met Dylan's gaze as it burned into hers.

His mouth pressed into a thin line. "Don't leave the room. I'll be by the bar if you need me." She nodded. Blowing out her breath, she turned - mind vacant of thought.

Brad stood just inside the entrance, arms crossed, and he watched Lexi as she moved toward him. Lexi reached him as the DJ shifted gears, and a rock anthem thumped through the room. Brad stepped toward her and cupped the back of her head, drawing her in for a kiss. "Enjoying yourself?"

Chilled by the memory of his last kiss, Lexi moved back from him and crossed her arms. "Yeah, it's a great night. What are you doing here?" Lexi asked.

"You invited me. Remember?" Brad said as he flipped the ticket out of his pocket. Then he raised an eyebrow. "Who'd know why? I mean, did you want me to see that?" he asked, gesturing to the dance floor.

A group of people bustled past them as they left the room, and Lexi moved aside. Brad's comment annoyed her, but she wouldn't show it. She lifted a shoulder. "What are you doing here, Brad?"

He frowned at the DJ before stepping toward her. "Look, can we talk somewhere quieter?"

She stiffened. Dylan's warning flashed through her mind. Brad stepped into her space again, and he slid an arm around her waist. Lexi sucked in a breath, pressing a hand against his chest. He smelled like alcohol, and she leaned back from him as more people stepped out of the room. She glanced toward the bar; photographers were vying for Dylan's attention.

"Please Lexi. Just give me five minutes."

Brad's arm around her waist held her closer as he whispered his plea, and she pressed another palm to his chest; her heart hammered as she looked back at his bleak and unfixed eyes. Suddenly the door behind them burst open and several people loudly entered, jostling them in the process, and Lexi felt herself being pulled from the room. As the door closed behind them and the chill of the air brushed her skin, she felt Brad's hand move from her waist and close around her arm. She pulled against him, though he barely slowed his pace. The sports center corridor, empty of persons, echoed with the clack of her heels and shaky commands for release.

Brad pushed through the exit doors and released Lexi with a shove. "Why did you want me to come tonight?" he asked, enunciating each word as he pressed a fist to his forehead.

Lexi glanced at her surroundings. A group of people stood nearby drinking; their laughter and spirited conversation providing a balm for the worry in her mind. Concerned about what she sensed from him, she reminded, "Ah, because, at the time, I wanted to share the evening with you. But we've since broken . . ." Brad moved towards her with such speed that she doubled backed, her words dissolving over her tongue.

"So, you did want me to see you all over him, *again*?" His voice raised with each word, and she felt the rough bricks of the Stadium wall pressed into her back, halting her retreat. Goosebumps raised over her skin, and she closed her eyes - praying for calm. When his hand gently cupped her face, she looked back at him. "You have made *such* a fool of me, Lexi." His voice, smooth once more as his thumb stroked her cheek, reminded her of the calm before the storm.

She glanced once more at the people nearby, they were finishing their drinks and moving back inside. Heart thumping, she looked back at Brad and flinched as he raised a hand, brushing her fringe aside. "But you know what? I've decided to forgive you. You know, like how you forgave me." His words annoyed her, but her conscious warned Lexi to hold her tongue. Still, when Brad tried to kiss her again, she turned her face away. She prayed that one of her friends noticed she was not inside anymore. Surely Dylan would have noticed by now? Fingers dug into her jaw as Brad forced her to look back at him before forcibly kissing her. Unable to free herself from his embrace, Lexi felt for the underside of his arms and pinched. Hard.

Brad drew back with a foul word and glared at her. His dark eyes widened as his pupils dilated, while he rubbed a hand under his triceps. Lexi glared back at him as she felt her mouth twitch into a snarl, her mind flashing back over the past months - and all the lies she'd believed that landed her here; the biggest almost cost her, her brother. "Shaun never hit you did he?"

A curt laugh answered her question, as Brad theatrically threw his arms in the air. "Oh, she's finally catching on!"

A cool chill worked its way into her bones at his words. This would end. Tonight. She took a bold step towards him. "Don't you dare come near me again. We are *over!*"

The wind rushed from her lungs as Brad slammed her back against the wall. His arm crushed her chest as he pinned her in place and she coughed, trying to regain her breath.

"Nobody ends a relationship with me, sweetheart," Brad whispered, his face mere inches from hers. "It's over when *I* say it is." He kissed her again, affirming his statement of possession

Fear speared Lexi's mind as he pinned her wrists by her side and pressed himself against her. A burst of adrenaline answered his assault, and Lexi swiftly lifted her knee into his groin.

He stumbled backward, and she watched in horror as his face contorted in various stages of agony. Willing herself to move while the opportunity presented itself, Lexi found she couldn't! Paralyzed by reality and the anger emanating from him, Lexi watched Brad draw back a closed fist, as if in slow motion. White light exploded in her vision, and she was thrown off balance into the stadium wall behind her before awkwardly collapsing to the footpath. Her face screamed in protest as she tried to roll onto her side. Her vision blurred and her head thumped with each pulse of her racing heart as she attempted to push herself up. A rough hand grasped her face, jerked her head upward, and she cried out. "Don't you pull a stunt like that again, understood?"

She stilled. Though she didn't recognize the menacing face before her, the voice triggered a memory. Tears slipped down her cheeks as fingernails bit into her jaw; she felt sick. "Baby . . ." the male before her said, his tone softening. "I don't want things to be this way between us." A kiss pressed to her lips, and Lexi pushed at him, trying to turn her face away. Whoever the man in front of her was, there was one thing she knew: he had hit her. All of a sudden she pitched forward as the hand gripping her jaw was torn away, and she buckled to the bitumen beneath her. Unable to control the shaking in her body, Lexi held a hand to her face while trying again to push herself up. A warm, tacky substance greeted her touch. A brawl broke out nearby, and Lexi strained to move away. But vertigo suddenly purged her stomach. Unable to bear the heavy tiredness closing in on her, Lexi slumped to the ground as the world went black.

THIRTY

"Move. Let me see her."

Frowning, Lexi tried to open her eyes. That new male voice was familiar. Large hands were encasing her head, and one of her eyes was forced open. She winced as a light flashed over her line of sight.

"She's concussed. I'm taking her home," the familiar voice said. A strong arm gently encircled her waist and drew her upward. Lexi's stomach lurched in response to the movement, and she shut her eyes. Voices around her added to the agony in her head. Unable to find her voice, she groaned.

"You're meant to be inside man. One of us can take her home."

"Concussed?! Are you serious?"

"I've seen it many times. She has a concussion, and I'm taking her home."

Someone made an incredulous sniff. "That must have been some hard knock he gave her. Lucky she's not unconscious."

"She's not far from it. Get her keys, please."

"Got them and her shoe too."

Were the people talking her friends? She felt dreamlike, and their voices were obscure in their hushed tones. Feeling off balance, she focused on trying to put one foot in front of the other. Pain shot up one of her legs, and Lexi slumped against the person holding her.

"Dylan this is crazy, you're the man of the hour in there. So, go back inside, and I'll take her."

"No."

"So, what? You just leave after everyone already knows you're here?"

"Hope, leave it! We can tell anyone who asks, something's come up, and he'll be back. Right man?"

"Right. Unlock the door please, Hope."

A car door opened and Lexi felt herself being lifted into the seat. Rolling her head back against the seat as the door shut her in, Lexi allowed the heaviness of sleep to pull her into its grasp once again.

* * * *

The sound of a car door closing roused Lexi, and she struggled to open her eyes as the door beside her opened. Lexi rolled her head to the side and forced her eyes to focus. Seeing Dylan beside her, she frowned, though she allowed him to help her out of the car. Her stomach rolled once again, and she leaned against him, breathing deeply until she was sure she wasn't going to be sick. Once the nausea passed, she inched back from him and raised her head to look at him. "I'm confused . . . about, why I'm here, and . . . why you are too."

Dylan's face was like stone in the cool light of the street lamp. "Lexi, do you know where you are?"

"Home," her voice squeaked, and she cleared her throat. The effort aggravated her headache, and she winced. "But not sure why. Isn't it the Vote Count thingy night?" Dylan glanced at the house then back at her. He looked unsure, and she forced her mind to focus. "What's wrong?"

"Nothing," he answered curtly, and she gasped as he scooped her up into his arms in one fluid motion and headed towards the house.

Once inside the moonlit sunken lounge room, Lexi slid from Dylan's arms onto the leather couch and laid back against the pillows - closing her eyes against the pain in her head. As his arm slipped out from under her, a warm earthy scent filled her nostrils, and she reached an arm out to him. "Wait."

"What is it?" he asked, hunkering next to the couch.

The memory was brief. If it was a memory - it could have been a dream for all her fuzzy mind recalled. Though something about his cologne triggered it, and Lexi had to know. Frowning, she sighed. "Did we, dance?" She opened her eyes to look at him and caught a subtle ache in his countenance moments before he dropped his head. Confusion mounted in her mind as she looked back at him waiting for an answer. Her curiosity heightened. When Dylan raised his head and looked back at her, she was struck by his serenity.

"Yeah," he whispered; a gentle smile curved his mouth as he looked back at her. "Yeah, we did."

She held his gaze. Something in his expression captivated her. Lexi had a vague awareness that Dylan needed to be somewhere else right now, though it seemed he was hesitating. Fighting her eyelids as they became heavier with each blink, she felt a glow spread throughout her body as the moment lengthened.

"Get some rest," he whispered. His voice was rough but comforting, and Lexi nodded, allowing her eyes to finally close. A rustle nearby told her he was rising, and while she wanted him to stay, sleep was pulling her in fast. When his cologne seemed to envelop her, her eyelids fluttered, struggling to open, and she lifted a hand weakly in search for him. When her fingers brushed his shirt, she drew in a sharp breath, amazed to find him near.

"I'll call in tomorrow, Lex. Goodnight." His lips pressed against her forehead and Lexi tensed, balling his shirt in her grasp. She peeled her eyes opened groggily and focused on him as he drew back. Wishing she could see him more clearly, Lexi released Dylan's shirt as hushed voices entered the room, and his gaze shifted from her to the doorway.

As the concerned faces of her parents filled her vision, Lexi closed her eyes again. Too tired to focus her mind any longer, she allowed sleep's grasp to pull her into its depths - the memory of Dylan's kiss still warming her skin.

THIRTY-ONE

An irritating beep disturbed Lexi's sleep, and once aware of it, consciousness began to dawn like a sunrise. Other things were now invading her peace: doors closing, muffled voices, and what was that smell? With great effort, Lexi opened her eyes and winced against the brightness in the room. Not knowing where she was, she looked around the sterile white room as the irritating beeping noise began speeding up. A familiar icy finger zipped up her spine as her mind registered where she was.

"Good morning, Lexi."

Her head whipped toward the male voice entering the room and she swallowed convulsively as he approached her bed.

He adjusted the stethoscope across the back of his neck and smiled. "You're anxious about why you're here? Just relax for me." He laid a light pressure to her shoulder.

Holding the man's gaze, Lexi laid back against the pillows. And, she finally realized the source of the beeping noise as the man moved to the end of her bed. "A . . . are you a d . . . doctor?" she asked, already sure of the answer.

"I am a doctor, Lexi. I'm the one who suggested that you remain with us when your parents brought you in last night." He looked at her over the clipboard, pen poised. "Do you remember?"

She counted her breaths in and out, willing her heart rate to slow, but her mind filled with snapshots of the night before. She dipped her head as everything became clear. She knew why she was in the hospital, and why her face and hip ached - why her arm was bandaged, and her ankle throbbed. She looked up at the doctor waiting patiently; her bottom lip quivered. "Yes, Doctor Leroux.

I remember."

He smiled and turned his probing eyes back to the clipboard. "Good. Now answer some questions for me, and let's see about getting you home."

* * * *

"Sweetie! How are you, I've been so worried!"

Switching her stare from the sunlit lawn to Hope, Lexi blinked slowly as her friend reclined next to her on the patio lounge. She waited while Hope looked her over. Lexi's mouth turned up in a crooked grin. "Is it bad?"

Hope hummed. "Do you want honest, or a sweet denial, sugar-coated answer?"

Movement in the house behind Hope caught Lexi's attention, and forgetting the question, found Shaun greeting her friends. As Nick and Trent stepped from the house, she watched Shaun clap Dylan on the shoulder, and they shared a laugh. She grimaced.

"How you doing champ?" Nick said with a grunt as he lowered himself onto the lounge opposite her.

Lexi raised her eyebrows sarcastically in answer at him as Trent sat down beside her.

"Ok," Trent gently said, "give us a look." Feeling her chin tilted towards him, Lexi didn't resist. As Trent looked over her face, his eyes lit tenderly, and he smiled. "You're still beautiful.

Closing her eyes, Lexi dropped her head. The door opened again, and hearing Dylan join them, she wiped her eyes and looked up. "You all didn't need to come around you know, I'm ok."

"After getting a message from your parents last night saying they'd taken you to the hospital, you'd better believe we'd be here!" Hope said.

Surprised, Lexi stared at Hope. "They messaged you? When?"

"A little after 10:00 p.m.," Hope replied, sharing a confused glance with the boys.

Lexi pursed her lips in thought. Absently she ran her fingers over the bandage on her arm, remembering the wall she fell against. "Wow, I must have been pretty messed up." The shadows dancing across the backyard drew her attention again. Lexi stared unblinkingly at them, thinking over the night before - all-the-while aware of the awkward silence settling over the group. Her heart felt heavy, her face throbbed, her hip ached, and her ankle was sprained. Yet, it was nothing compared to the dull sensation in her mind. Unable to believe what her memory recalled of the night before, Lexi tried to dismiss the kaleidoscope of images as nothing more than bad dreams. But when Lexi's eyes fell upon the reddened marks that covered Dylan's knuckles, a new memory surfaced. Dylan looked up at her, and her body warmed unexpectedly.

"So why did they take you to the hospital in the end?" Nick asked.

Tearing her eyes from Dylan, Lexi took a deep breath and lifted a shoulder. "Just a precaution. Mum was worried that my speech was a bit funny. And apparently, I had some memory loss. I just remember being really tired."

Trent shifted in his seat. "So, you remember last night?"

Glancing back at Dylan, Lexi caught him watching her with more than casual interest. Was he hoping she remembered, or not? "Every bit," she answered steadily, noting the way Dylan's eyes darkened. When a hand slapped her leg lightly, she flinched. Turning to Hope, she encountered her friend smiling brightly back at her.

"That's fabulous news, hun!"

"Why?" Lexi asked. "Fabulous that I remember being assaulted? Fabulous that I can't bear to look at myself in the mirror? Fabulous that any moment I could have a flashback? Is it fabulous that . . ." "Lexi," Trent said, cutting her off.

His voice was firm and warning in its tone, but she ignored him. Disbelief gave way to anger, and she felt her eyes well as her voice caught. "Is it fabulous that my professor won't give me another extension for tomorrow, so I have to face a whole auditorium – something that already scares me to death – looking like this!" Gesturing to her face, Lexi slumped against the cushions. Her fierce demeanor dissolved against her will, and she dropped her head into her hand.

"Lexi."

"Trent, I don't want to hear it, ok?" Lexi said from behind her hand, focusing on calming herself and reining in her emotions. Even though she was upset, her friends didn't deserve to wear it. "I'm sorry guys, but I just can't understand why God would let this happen to me. What on earth have I done to deserve this?"

"*Lexi!*" Trent said, interrupting her once again, and the tone in his voice told her to listen. She raised her head and dropped her arm limply into her lap. His features were stern though his eyes were alight. Suddenly she regretted her outburst. "It is not *God's* will that this happened to you. He lets things happen to teach, shape, or direct us. You need to decide if you're going to let God use what happened to you for good, or if you're going to let anger reign and destroy yourself by it."

She knew Trent was right and hung her head, ashamed of herself. "I'm sorry. I'm just such a mess at the moment . . . I dunno what's going on." Her words hung like a black cloud over them in the silence that followed, and she knew she should pray, but nothing came to mind. She needed to be alone to prepare for the presentation tomorrow – or at least try too. A chair scraped back from the table, and she heard someone rising. Looking up she saw Nick collecting his things.

"Guys, I think we should leave, and let Lexi have some time. It's been an intense twenty-four hours for her."

One by one they agreed with Nick's suggestion, and she watched as her friends rose to leave. She wanted them to stay, but she couldn't deny the desire she had to be alone. Maybe a bubble bath after they'd left would improve her mood? Thoughts of a steamy bath, filled with her coconut and vanilla soaking salts, tempted Lexi as she walked her friends to the door. She hugged each of them as they filed out.

Dylan lagged behind. Once they were alone, Lexi turned to him. There was restrained energy about him as he looked back at her, and her stomach quivered oddly. Lexi hugged herself as her arms crossed her body.

"You ok?" he asked, plunging his hands into his jean pockets.

Lexi's breath came raggedly as she drew it in, and she shrugged. "Guess we'll find out tomorrow."

THIRTY-TWO

*D*ust motes suspended in the sunlit hallway outside the auditorium provided a much-needed distraction for Lexi while she waited. Beyond the double doors behind her, lay her worst nightmare - a room full of scrutinizing peers and professors.

After several failed attempts to disguise the bruising over her face and scratches along her jaw, Lexi had given up and fallen into despair. People gawked as they passed by her in the hallway, enhancing her feelings as a freak sideshow. All she wanted to do was go back to bed. All her fingernails had been chewed off, and her water bottle nearly emptied while she waited. Still, time continued to tick by at an agonizingly slow pace.

Hope's parting words from the day before echoed in her mind, and she took a long breath in and let it out slowly. *"Just breathe, Lexi,"* Hope had said. Well, she was trying! The frustration at her professor for refusing an extension was like a vise crushing her chest, though she refused to give him the satisfaction of failing her.

Her phone vibrated in her bag, and she grabbed at it- desperate for a distraction. Seeing a message from Dylan, a smile lit her features as she opened the text.

'Good luck, Lex. Will be praying for you. D.'

Muffled applause sounded from behind the double doors, and her blood pressure dropped. Tipping the dregs from her water bottle into her mouth, Lexi fired a message back: *'Thanks, I need it!'*

As the doors beside her opened and her professor stepped out, she rose from the bench seat and greeted him. His gaze lingered, and she looked squarely back at him. "Good. He looks uncomfortable," she thought. Well, he can remain uncomfortable for making her come in after what she'd been through. Satisfied when he looked away, Lexi moved past him and into the auditorium as her phone vibrated again. She reached the stage as the Master of Ceremonies introduced her to the audience. With trepidation, Lexi climbed the stairs, and she approached the podium.

Unlike at the concert, with lights in her eyes, Lexi found that she could see each individual face fixed on her own. She could see those sharing whispers, and those who made the coughing sounds when her silence lengthened. She could see her professor check his watch with unnecessary exaggeration at the rear of the room, and the graders before her with their pens poised. She felt a blackness threatening her peripheral vision. Needing a distraction, Lexi tilted the phone towards her to check the time, and she saw a flashing envelope on the screen. Remembering a text had come through, she pretended she was organizing her notes but ran her eyes over Dylan's message. *"Just be yourself. 2 Tim 1:7. x"*

Lexi knew the verse well and having it sent to her at this moment, released the pressure within her chest. God was with her and Lexi knew what to do. She straightened herself up and grasped the podium. As Lexi looked around the room, she started her presentation off with her testimony on overcoming fear, surviving abuse, and holding God to His promises. When she noticed that bodies were leaning forward in their seats, and the whispered conversations ceased, she grew bolder, stepping away from the podium. Diligently, Lexi tried to make eye contact with everyone present. By the time she'd flicked the last slide up showing the community they were raising money for, Lexi had the audience captivated; when she concluded her presentation with how much money was raised, the audience applauded. Lexi's breath raced out as she smiled, accepting their approval of her speech with a dip of her head. Then she looked on in amazement as one by one, the audience rose to their feet.

Lexi's cheeks bloomed with color as she collected her papers. Relieved, she made her way off stage and toward the familiar fluorescent green sign. Along the way, she noticed a few girls rise to their feet and make their way toward the exit. Not thinking much of it, Lexi pushed through the doors that led to the hallway and came face to face with the other girls. "Hi," Lexi said, intending to pass them by, but one moved into her path.

"Sorry, could I have a quick sec, Lexi?" The young girl's voice was high pitched and held a tremor, but the determination in her eyes was what caught Lexi's attention.

She halted. "Sure, what's up?" Lexi asked softly. The other girls swiftly came alongside the one who spoke, faces beaming as they elbowed their friend. Lexi moved her books from one hip to the other while she waited for the girl who appeared desperate to say something. But the other student either couldn't find the words or didn't know how to express herself. Lexi understood that feeling well.

The young girl glanced at her friends, then took a deep breath. "Um, I just wanted to say, how much of an inspiration you are to me."

Shocked, Lexi looked at the young girl. Questions came to mind fast, but a small voice within warned Lexi to keep silent and to let the girl speak.

"Tell her what you want to tell her," the dark headed girl next to her said, her eyes darting to Lexi while elbowing her friend.

She gazed up, and Lexi was struck by the earnest look in her eyes. "I'm Kate, and I had a boyfriend who hurt me earlier this year. I couldn't leave my room for months! These are my friends, Evie and Laura, and they helped me a lot! But, to see you up there giving a speech so confidently, so soon after what happened to you . . . it gave me hope for the first time - hope that maybe I could get back to who I used to be. You know, before what happened to me."

Lexi looked back at her, at a loss for words. The girl's humility was rare, and Lexi took a few steps back and sat on the bench nearby. Kate soon joined Lexi while her friends remained standing. The afternoon passed quickly as she listened to Kate talk out her experiences and explain her struggle to overcome the abuse. What struck Lexi most was Kate's perseverance in rebuilding her faith and trust in people. As Lexi listened, a thought materialized and blurred her vision with tears. For years Lexi had prayed for confidence and direction, and the call that appeared in her mind so abruptly was unmistakable. With a grateful heart, Lexi bowed her head and quietly acknowledged the gentle nudge of the Savior while a tear slipped down her cheek.

"Why are you crying?" Kate asked.

Without a second thought, Lexi pulled a notepad and pen out of her bag. "You have no idea what an answer to prayer you have been to me, Kate. Here is my number, my address, and the church I attend." Taking Kate's hand, unable to reign in her smile, she sighed. "I would love it if you would stay in touch." Rising, Lexi handed Kate the piece of paper and apologized for having to cut their chat short.

Kate nodded and tucked the piece of paper into her bag, "I will. See you again soon, Lexi. And, thanks again."

THIRTY-THREE

Arriving early for the Leadership Team meeting, as requested by Dave, Lexi and Hope let themselves into the church hall to set up. While Lexi switched on lights and unlocked doors, Hope went for the sporting equipment and pulled out a basketball. Despite Hope's claims of needing exercise, Lexi knew there was more to her interest in the upcoming basketball season: Shaun.

"So, how'd you go?" Hope asked tossing Lexi the basketball.

"It was . . . interesting." Lexi said, rolling the ball over in her hands. As Lexi lined up a shot, she shook her head in wonder, remembering the afternoon she'd had. Grinning, Lexi pushed aside her suspicious thoughts about Hope. Still amazed, she let the ball go, watched as it sailed through the air and swished through the net. "You know that feeling you get when you know your life is never going to be the same again?" Lexi asked dreamily.

Hope chuckled, nodding her head. "I certainly do. What happened to you?"

Catching the ball as Hope tossed it back, Lexi bounced it hand to hand thinking over the afternoon and how best to explain.

"So, tell me what happened then," Hope prompted, impatience nipping at her words.

Still trying to find the right words as the hall doors opened, Lexi tossed Hope the ball. When Nick and Dylan entered midargument, Lexi suggested, "Ah, how about we catch up for a drink afterward and go sort these boys out?" Hope agreed, but Lexi heard her friend's frustrated sigh from the other side of the Key. The topic of the boy's heated discussion made Lexi giggle, and she shared a look with Hope as they stood nearby watching them, waiting for a chance to interject.

"Think they'd notice if I tossed it at one of their heads?" Hope quietly asked as she spun the ball atop one of her fingers.

The hall door banged closed again, and Lexi turned to see Dave enter as the boys fell silent.

"What are you boys arguing about?" Dave asked as he strode towards them, his stern voice echoing off the walls.

Nick sighed; irritation clear at the request to explain himself. "Dylan's trying to argue the animals that went onto Noah's ark *weren't* two by two. But everyone knows they all went on two by . . ."

"It's right there, Nick. I'm not making it up!" Dylan said. chuckling as he shook his head in disbelief. "Some went on by sevens!" Aware that Dylan was right, Lexi looked to Dave to see how he would solve the issue.

Dave pulled his Bible out from under his arm and flipped it open. He looked as if he was about to speak when he grinned and shut the book again. "No, I have a better idea." Dave moved away, gesturing for everyone to follow. Nestled on the stage couches ten minutes later, Lexi watched as Dave wheeled out the whiteboard, then looked at them. "I wanted you all to meet me in the hall for our Leadership Team meeting tonight, as I wanted to run through a game idea with you. However, in the wake of this issue between two of our leaders," Dave said with an accusing glance at Nick and Dylan, "I think we'll do a game called 'Acting out' on Friday. We'll break into five teams – one team for each of you to lead – and we'll give each team a story from the Bible to act out - like charades." He pulled the pen lid off the marker and poised it over the whiteboard. "It'll also help you guys to learn your Bibles a bit better too. Ok, let's go."

Through laughter and discussion, four stories were soon written up on the board. Only one more remained, and it was Nick's turn to choose what story he wanted. He sat forward in his seat, though before he could speak, Dave wrote: "Noah and the flood." Dylan barked out a laugh and clapped his hands, only to receive a sharp jab in the arm from Nick. Dave turned, recapping his pen and looked at Nick with an expression welcoming complaint. When Nick slouched back in the armchair, Dave's expression softened as he picked up his Bible. "Genesis 7:2-3, Nick. Have a read before Friday."

* * * *

Still buzzing with the new and exciting sense of direction, Lexi burst through the front door eager to share the news with her family. A raised voice from the kitchen made Lexi draw up short. For a moment, she debated whether to go to her room to research the idea she had, or head to the kitchen to see what the fuss was about. Curiosity won, and she turned towards the kitchen.

"What did you honestly expect I'd do?" Shaun's voice was furious.

The hair on the back of Lexi's neck rose at the sound of her brother's vehemence. With carefully placed steps, Lexi cringed as she tip-toed the rest of the way down the hallway and peered into the open living area.

Shaun paced while he spoke on his phone. "My decision stands, take it as far as you like." He turned unexpectedly and looked squarely at Lexi.

She straightened, eyes wide as if she'd been caught red-handed, and looked back at her brother as he finished his phone call.

"Tell him, I'll be at the meeting. Monday morning, at 9:00 a.m." Shaun slammed the phone down, and she jumped.

A question burned in her mind, but unsure how it would be received, Lexi took an uneven breath before she ventured into the room. "What was that about?"

Caged lions were more relaxed than Shaun, and Lexi bit her lip. When Shaun sat down heavily at the dining room table, he ran a hand over his hair and looked at her wearily. 'I fired Brad, and the Union is trying to claim unfair dismissal. Just extra stress I don't need."

Her legs felt like lead as she digested the information. Lexi walked unsteadily towards the dining table and sat down opposite him. Shaun looked up as she sat, and Lexi knew he was taking in the marks on her face. She dropped her head.

"He really made a mess of you, you know that."

Lexi felt heat pour into her face, and she regretted her curiosity as the exhilaration she'd felt most of the day vanished. Thoughtfully, she acknowledged the reality check, and she dipped her head. "Momentarily, yes I guess he did."

Silence hung in the room like a lead weight between them, mirrored only by the heaviness Lexi felt in her heart. How could she repair the breech between them? "I know you didn't hit Brad, now." Lexi offered weakly.

Shaun sat back in his seat and breathed a deep sigh, his expression strained. "All this could have been avoided you know?"

"I know."

"You could have been seriously hurt."

Lexi drew in a sharp breath. Her eyes stung as memories flooded back, and she couldn't speak past the lump in her throat. Nightmares had been constantly reminding her of that fact.

"Have you made a statement to the police yet?" Shaun's flat tone broke into her inward thoughts and dread curled anew in Lexi's stomach, she shuddered. "Not yet."

"Might be a good idea while you still look the way you do, don't you think? No point going when your face is all healed up is there?"

Unwilling to consider giving a statement to police and rehashing things she was trying to forget, Lexi decided a change of topic was in order. She cleared her throat. "So, where's mum and dad?"

"Playing pool with the next door neighbors." He held her gaze; jaw set.

Her ploy to change the subject backfired. Unable to decide if Shaun was angry with her or the situation at work, Lexi wondered whether to try and discuss it or not. Before she could make up her mind, the decision was made; Shaun rose, collected his diary and phone from the kitchen table, then strode from the room.

He paused in the doorway, and glanced back at her over his shoulder. "Make sure you see the cops this week."

THIRTY-FOUR

"*I*t's not as bad as you're making it out to be," Nick said. "I'll meet you at the station for the appointment time, and all will be ok. I promise."

Lexi stared into her cup of tea as she dunked the tea bag over and over. She listened intently while Nick explained the process of making a statement. If it weren't for Nick's insistence and her brother's wishes, she'd have just let it go. The bruises were an ugly faded color of yellows and browns tinted with lilac now. And, the nail scratch marks around her jaw were thin scabs about to fall off. Another few days, and a little makeup would cover all the evidence of the night she hoped to soon forget. However, the doctor's script for counseling sat on the bench was demand for attention. Lexi pushed the script out of her line of sight and removed the tea bag from her cup, before crossing the kitchen to get the milk. "How can you promise, Nick? Have you done this before?"

Nick cleared his throat, "Lexi, do you remember that little place I went to for three months not that long ago?"

She placed the milk carton on the bench with a thud. His sarcasm was not what she wanted. "I know you're almost a policeman, Nick. But have you ever had to do one of these statement things?"

"No," he answered simply. "But I've taken statements."

"Mock ones?"

"Does it matter?"

Lexi felt her knuckles turn white as she gripped the phone. "Yes, it does! To me!"

Nick sighed. His voice turned soothing, and she knew he was pulling on his training to talk her through it. "Ok, Lexi. Yes, they were mock interviews. They're designed to give us real-life experiences so we can serve better. Listen, I'll come over shortly and pick you up. I'll take you to the station, then once we're finished, how about a little visit to someone's favorite ice cream parlor?"

A smile curled one side of Lexi's mouth. "Is bribery in the book too?" Nick sniffed, and Lexi knew he was smiling. His helpful offer made her feel better.

"Depends. Is it working?" Nick asked lightly.

She jumped up to sit on the kitchen counter and sighed. Resigned to what she had to do, she encouraged herself with the fact it would be another piece of life experience she could pass onto others one day. "Yes, it's working." She blew her breath out. "Ok, I can do this. Will you be in the interview room with me though?"

The doorbell chimed through the house, and Lexi jumped off the bench. Craning her neck down the hallway, she wondered who would call by in the middle of a workday.

"Yes you can, and yes I will be." Nick chuckled. "I'll be around shortly."

Nick hung up, and Lexi replaced the phone in its cradle as the doorbell chimed again. Remembering her Jeep was in the driveway, she went to answer the door, knowing it was useless to pretend nobody was home. Catching her reflection in the coat stand mirror, Lexi halted a moment before opening the door. The bruising on her face was highlighted grotesquely by the afternoon sun, and she wrinkled her nose. While she was adapting to her appearance, it would be shocking to a visitor. Quickly ruffling her hair so that more of her auburn waves disguised the affected side of her face, she turned to the door and opened it with a smile. A cry of anguish followed, and she tried to close the door, but a foot fell in its path.

"Lexi, please. I need to talk to you," Brad said, his voice desperate.

Hot tears burned Lexi's eyes, and she pushed vainly against the door, but her limbs were weak with fear. It was a dream. A nightmare. Brad couldn't possibly be shadowing her doorstep. Pressure was laid against the door, and Lexi gave up, her arms falling limply to her sides as she staggered backward and sunk down onto the staircase behind her. What was the point? He had her beat at every turn. Curling her arms over her head, she begged God to do something, anything! She heard Brad hunker down in front of her, and she shrank back. However, his strong fingers curled under her wrists, and he pulled her arms away from her head. Lexi snatched her limbs back and pushed herself away from him – suddenly cornered against the staircase railings. Her body shook uncontrollably as she watched him through unblinking eyes.

Brad moved to sit next to her on the stairs. "Lexi I wish you'd just relax a moment and talk to me." She flinched as he went to touch her leg, and she heard him sigh. He turned to her and leaning in, placed an arm on the stairs behind her. "Ok, if you won't talk, just listen then. Last Saturday night, I'd been out with the boys drinking, then I saw you with him again, and I don't know what got into me." Brad touched her hair, and Lexi batted his hand away. He cleared his throat, shifting closer. "I am trying to apologize. The least you could do is acknowledge me."

Lexi felt her stomach lurch as she pressed herself further into the railings. She hid her face from him, even though Brad tried to catch her gaze. When his fingers slid under her arm to bodily turn her toward him, Lexi attempted to snatch her arm back. However, Brad held it more firmly. Mustering all her strength, Lexi tugged her arm free. But Brad grabbed her again, twisted her face toward him, and pinned her arm back on the step behind her. Adrenaline exploded inside her, and Lexi slapped him with her free hand. Brad's eyes blackened in a heartbeat as he caught her wrist. Lexi recoiled and closed her eyes.

"HEY!" Nick's voice boomed in the entryway.

Brad's weight shifted from her suddenly, and Lexi opened her eyes. Nick blocked the doorway as Brad stepped up to him. Lexi watched from the corner of her eye, while wild visions of what might happen crashed through her mind.

"What do you think you're doing here, mate?" Nick questioned, his feet planted to the spot, unmoved by attempted intimidation.

Nick's eyes were cold, and Lexi trembled, while goosebumps prickled her skin.

"Well, that's really none of your business, is it?" Brad countered, making no attempt to leave.

Nick grinned, his head tilted back in a display of confidence and ownership of the situation. "Tell you what, you leave now, and you *might* not have a record as your shadow for the next twenty years."

Another wave of nausea crashed over Lexi. Distraught, she covered her mouth and turned away. Her trembling muscles ached, and Lexi felt drained as the earlier burst of adrenaline faded. The front door slammed, and she jumped. Turning, she saw Nick striding toward her moments before being wrapped in his arms. Some time passed before she felt his arms loosen. Sitting back, Lexi raised her head to look at him. His eyes still held the same cold steel appearance as he seemed to be examining her. Though he was relaxed, she knew he was still alert.

He cleared his throat. "We can cancel the statement interview if you want."

Lexi shook her head and wiped her eyes. "No. I have to do this," she said, "I won't let him beat me."

Nick nodded and stood, offering a hand to her. Sure her stomach had settled, Lexi took his arm and rose unsteadily to her feet. With a measured gait, she stepped off the stairs and crossed the landing toward the front door. Nick stopped at the door to open it, and he paused, a grin played upon his mouth. "How about we add harassment to the list of charges while we're there, shall we?"

THIRTY-FIVE

The street Nick turned onto was all too familiar to Lexi, and nowhere near the ice cream parlor that she was longing for. She looked over at him. "Why are we going to Hope's place?"

Nick grinned. His eyes remained on the road as he reached for the radio and turned the volume up. "Hey, this is a great song!"

With a shake of her head, Lexi turned to look out the window and huffed with exaggeration. "And, here I was innocently thinking you were taking me out to the ice cream parlor after that . . . ordeal."

"Trust me, Lexi, this will be better," Nick said.

As he pulled into Hope's driveway, Lexi recognized several extra vehicles, and she couldn't help the grin that spread over her face. It was clear something had been organized without her knowing, though as long as ice cream was on offer, she didn't mind one bit.

Lexi thanked Nick for holding the door for her and stepped out into the Meyer's backyard. Wide-eyed Lexi took it all in - fairy lights flickered above a giant screen set up over the BBQ; and couches, bean bags, and pillows were strewn over the patio floor where the outdoor table usually sat. Trent and Dylan sat engaged in a deep conversation, while Hope sorted cables between the projector and the laptop. Hope glanced up as Nick shut the door.

"This is awesome," Lexi said, looking back at Nick.

"Told you it was better than a cold ice cream parlor," Nick said, his smile warm.

"You're here!" Hope called out, drawing Lexi's attention back to the group. Hope waved her over with both hands. "Come on. Come on. Come on, we've been waiting for you!"

Moments later from an over cushioned sofa, Lexi watched Hope make the final adjustments to whatever was on the laptop.

Positioned proudly in front of the screen, Hope gestured around the yard and smiled. "Ok, hun. This is a little indulgence I got for myself. And, after the week you've had, I wanted to create a little chill out time for you too." Hope nodded at something over Lexi's shoulder.

Lexi looked behind her and spotted Nick coming out of the house carrying a box of her favorite ice cream. Speechless, she turned back to Hope.

"So," Hope continued, "I've gathered some happy things for you: a few of your favorite movies, favorite ice cream flavors, and your favorite take away should arrive in about an hour. Oh, and us – your favorite people!"

Unable to reign in her smile, Lexi accepted the ice cream Nick handed her before he offered the box to the others. This was exactly what she needed. With a heart full of thanks to God for her friends, Lexi elbowed Hope as she nestled in beside her. "Thank you for this."

"You're welcome, sweetie," Hope whispered. "Now shhh, the movie is starting."

The movie was one of Lexi's favorites. However, she couldn't focus as she mulled over the repercussions of the statement she made to the police, the restraining order, and the likely outcome of Shaun's meeting with the Union. Chewing her lip, Lexi became aware of eyes upon her. She glanced around the room to find Dylan looking at her, a question reflected in his expression. Lexi tilted her head at him, and Dylan subtly shook his head before he turned back to the screen. Her stomach quivered oddly again, and Lexi tried to focus on the movie; however, her mind turned inward. Intuition said that Dylan wanted to talk to her, and while she expected it, Lexi wasn't sure if she was ready for that conversation.

The evening passed quickly, and the food Hope ordered in left them all feeling satisfied and sleepy. With effort, Lexi placed her plate on the coffee table and stretched her arms overhead. "I'm going to head off, Hope. It's been a big day, and I'm wrecked," Lexi said, muffling a yawn.

Hope scrambled from the seat and made for the projector. "No, no. Just one more movie! I saved the best for last."

Trent rose and placed his plate and cup in a nearby bin. "I'm with Lexi. I'm sorry Hope, I've got an early start tomorrow, so I better get going."

Hope pouted as Trent said his goodbye's and headed back to the house. As the door shut behind him, she asked, "Anybody else want to leave?"

Soft snoring interrupted their intermission, and Lexi looked around in the low light to find Nick asleep in one of the bean bags. "Well, pop the next movie on. Looks like I'm staying a bit longer, my ride's fallen asleep."

Hope's face brightened in an instant, and she knelt down to change the disc in the laptop. When Hope's mobile rung, she rose and walked at pace back to the house, excited laughter trailing behind her.

Eyebrows raised, Lexi wondered who was on the phone when she noticed Dylan rise to approach her. She greeted him with a smile even though she tensed as he lowered himself to sit beside her. The new and unnerving sensation of Dylan's hip against hers almost launched her from the sofa. He smelled like diesel and workshop grease, and a heavy awareness of him began to radiate through Lexi's body. Desperate for a distraction, Lexi tried to focus on the movie playing, but her eyes fell upon Dylan's hands wrapped around the drink he was holding. As she took in the oil-stained lengths of his well-formed fingers, Lexi noticed the bruising over his knuckles was gone. Lexi found herself thrilled by knowing how they'd become bruised! She closed her eyes tightly and sat forward. What was she thinking?!

Dylan cleared his throat. "That would be Josh on the phone."

"Josh? Football Josh?" Lexi asked, her voice breathy as she tried an easy glance over her shoulder at Dylan. A grin curled on his unshaven face, and Dylan dipped is head. Lexi's throat dried up, and she popped an M&M into her mouth before sinking back into the sofa. "Unbelievable."

"So, how are you doing anyway?" he asked, nudging her with his shoulder. "Nick told us you had a visitor this afternoon." Lexi stared at the chocolates laying in her palm. "Yeah."

"You ok?"

There was more to Dylan's question than just a friend's inquiry, and Lexi threw back the rest of the M&M's before she shifted her body toward him. "Um, no. I completely lost it." Her shoulders slumped, and she lowered her head as the memory of the counseling script on the kitchen bench at home came back to her. "I think something is very wrong with me. I've never behaved like that before," Lexi quietly said.

Dylan shifted in his seat, and Lexi glanced at him as he threw an arm over the back of the couch and shifted his body toward her. "Nothing is wrong with you," he said. "You've been abused, then harassed by an ex. How would you expect yourself to act?"

Lexi shook her head. Just thinking about how she reacted made her feel stupid. Positive she had more control than that, Lexi sniffed in annoyance as she looked over at the bowl of M&M's. "I don't know, Dylan, maybe a bit more normal to start with." A light touch against her hair stilled her thoughts, and Lexi felt her skin warm. Her chocolate craving disappeared, and she turned her gaze back to Dylan, making no attempt to move away from him this time.

Dylan's gentle cobalt eyes, backlit by the flicking lights above, fixed on her as his fingers brushed Lexi's fringe aside. Softly he trailed a path lightly down the fading bruises on her cheek. "There is nothing wrong with you," he said quietly. "Another couple of days and these marks will be gone. The memory will fade too."

Lexi's chest tightened. Positive that she was not alone with the turn in their friendship, Dylan's words gave her hope for tomorrow, and she responded to that unspoken possibility. "Then what?" she asked, her voice no more than a whisper.

His eyes flickered as if in conflict before he tipped her chin towards him. "Well then, in time, Lex, you'll make new memories."

She heard the suggestion behind Dylan's words, and a rush of hopefulness flooded her body as he leaned in. Never had she imagined him in this way.

"Dylan! I. Love. You!" Hope's shrill voice broke the atmosphere.

Lexi sat immobilized in her seat while she tried to steady her breathing. Dylan slowly sat back from her. When he turned to Hope, Lexi could see the pulse that hammered in his throat, and she blinked. As Hope slumped into the chair opposite them, she appeared unable to contain her happiness. Cheerfully she threw a chip at Dylan. Confused, Lexi looked between the two of them when Dylan casually picked up the chip that had tumbled down his shirt and ate it. "So, I'm guessing that was Josh?"

Hope nodded and smiled like a Cheshire cat. "Yes! I owe you big time!"

"Can everybody keep it down a little? I'm trying to sleep over here."

Remembering Nick, Lexi shot Dylan a concerned look, and he subtly shook his head.

Dylan rose and laid a foot in the side of Nick's bean bag. "Come on buddy, let's leave these ladies to it. Hope, you're welcome. See you all at the game?"

"Oh, we'll be there!" Hope sang as she flicked her legs over the arm of the chair.

Lexi nodded and smiled despite the unsettled sensation within her. "Wouldn't miss it!" Lexi shakily said, and she reached for some more M&M's.

No sooner had the door shut behind the boys and Hope plopped on the sofa next to her. "Ok, what did I just interrupt?" Surprised, Lexi hadn't expected Hope to notice anything in her euphoric state.

Hope grinned back knowingly. "Don't you give me that look, woman. I could cut the atmosphere out here with a knife when I came back out. What's going on?"

Taking a calming breath, Lexi heard the words in her mind before she said them, and her body warmed deliciously in response. Touching a cool hand to her burning cheeks, still feeling the trace of Dylan's fingers against her skin, she grinned at Hope. "I think . . . I think Dylan was about to kiss me."

Hope's eyes widened as she sat back on the sofa. Then she bounced up from the pillows, twisted herself to land cross-legged in front of Lexi, and laid both hands on Lexi's arm. "Ok, tell me everything."

THIRTY-SIX

The afternoon sun beat down, and Lexi pushed her sunglasses up on her nose, wishing she'd brought a hat as well. Splashes of red with white and blue with gold decorated the grounds, the stands, and the lawn in readiness for the Grand Final. More and more cars lined the perimeter of The Valley football ground as she watched.

An elbow in her ribs drew Lexi's attention from the crowds to Hope. Her friend pointed with enthusiasm toward the Tiger's race. "There he is!"

Lexi craned her neck and caught sight of Josh Anderson jogging onto the field with the Tigers, but someone else soon held her attention. Her stomach fluttered as she watched Dylan, thankful for the sunglasses disguising the direction of her gaze. She leaned into Hope. "So, what's the deal with you and Josh?"

Hope laughed, the sound like songbirds in the morning. "Oh, let's just say I have a little date tonight after the game. And just so you know, I know your attention is elsewhere at the moment."

Smiling at Hope over her sunglasses, Lexi realized she'd underestimated her best friend. "Ok, fine, guilty! I'm just trying to work things out."

Hope sipped her cappuccino. "Any luck?"

Lexi shook her head. Dylan was one of her closest friends, and he had been for a long time. So, the feelings he'd roused in her over the last week left Lexi wondering how to act around him. Should she ask him about it or ignore it? Though she had tried hard not to read anything into their recent encounters, each day the feelings were getting harder to ignore.

Trent and Nick rejoined the girls after their trip to the Coffee Van. A sigh of relief gushed out of Lexi as she listened into their conversation about personal abilities and strengths. Finally, a topic she could discuss.

"No way, Nick. Trent is a shepherd. He looks after us and keeps us in line," Hope said as she leaned over Lexi to emphasize her opinion.

Nick's gaze traveled casually over the game in progress before he returned Hope's attention, "I'm not saying he isn't. I'm just saying I think he's got a few other aces up his sleeve as well."

Trent held a hand up and grinned. "It's an arguable point guys because I haven't figured it out myself yet. But I can say, I have my suspicions. Just waiting on God to reveal His plan for me now. What about you Hope, why do you think you were asked to be on the Leadership Team?"

Chin propped in her palm, Hope leaned forward and raised her eyebrows. She shrugged. "I have no idea either! But I know I'm having a lot of fun!"

"You're pretty musical, Hope," Trent said. "Maybe your gift is music?"

199

"You've also got a rock-solid faith there, girl. So, maybe it's faith?" Nick said, plunging his hand into a bag of chips.

Lexi glanced at Nick. "What about you Nick? Do you have any idea?"

Nick looked over the game again and watched as the visiting team kicked a goal. "If you'd asked me before I went to the Academy, I would have said I had no idea. But now, I'm confident that it's to serve and encourage. To help build the kids up and grow their confidence and all that."

"I reckon that's Dylan too," Trent added, as he watched the game.

Following Trent's line of vision, Lexi watched Dylan pat a few of his teammates on the back and appear to instruct others. Her stomach flipped again. She turned back to the conversation and nodded at Trent's assessment. "I agree with you there, Trent. Dylan is definitely an encourager."

"What about you, sweetie?" Hope asked her as she finished her cappuccino.

Lexi stared into her drink and grinned. Here was the moment she'd been waiting for: to share the changes she'd discovered about herself. She brushed the fringe from her eyes and took a deep breath. "Well, I've been waiting to share this, but I never knew how to bring the topic up."

They were all watching her. She knew it. She felt it. She just needed the right words to explain what she had discovered. "Well, like Trent, I'm still praying about this, but the undeniable impression I've had is that my place is in Leadership. It hit me like a ton of bricks after the presentation on Monday." With a deep breath, Lexi explained everything from the beginning - how she conducted the presentation and how the girls caught up with her afterward. She shared the burden she felt to speak in the youth sector about abusive relationships. Lexi felt called to help young people recognize the signs of a dangerous relationship and equip them with the skills to break free. More importantly, Lexi wanted to give them the knowledge needed to heal afterward. "I know this is strange coming from me guys. You've all seen me freak out in front of audiences so I cannot believe I'm saying these things. But I can't deny it," Lexi said, rolling the contents of her drink around. "I've even enrolled in our local Toastmasters!"

"Since when? Monday?" Hope asked, her pretty face distorted with confusion.

Lexi grinned at her friend and nodded. "Yeah. I came home from Uni on Monday, researched it, prayed about it, and then booked myself a seat on Tuesday. I'll be going along as a guest to one of their get-togethers. See how that goes, then I guess I'll sign up as a member."

Trent removed his sunglasses and looked at Lexi as if they were playing cards and he knew she was holding the card he wanted. Sunlight illuminated the hypnotic power of Trent's green eyes. "What's your goal with this new direction?"

"Aside from public speaking, I'd also like to do counseling," Lexi answered, and her voice caught as the last words escaped unbidden. Her friend's faces morphed from surprise, to wonder, to concern, and Lexi wanted to dispel any worries they had. As she opened her mouth to explain, she was drowned out by the half time siren. Noise from the crowd grew audibly as people raced onto the cleared oval or lined up outside food vans. Waiting for the noise to settle, Lexi noticed as Nick leaned over Trent. "What did you say, Nick?"

"I said: I think you're on the right path. You've got first-hand experience in the field you want to speak in, and judging by the youth at our church, you'll always have a captive audience." Nick dipped his head, "You've got my vote girl, go get 'em!" Trent patted Lexi's back and echoed Nick's comments.

She smiled at the boys and thanked them for their support before turning to Hope. The young woman wore her trademark, megawatt smile as she laid her hand upon Lexi's arm. "All I can say is, wow. You've floored me with this one, but you know, I think it fits. The youth love you, and they hang on every word you say . . .

not that I think you've noticed," Hope finished, nudging her with her shoulder.

Closing her eyes, Lexi bowed her head. She hadn't noticed the youth group's response. More often than not she'd been too concerned with remaining unnoticed. But in hindsight, she could see that the kids responded well to her and swamped her at youth nights. They all seemed to vie for her attention, and Lexi remembered their excitement when she was named one of the new leaders.

As the Tigers ran back onto the field for the second half, Lexi put the whirling thoughts away and focused on the game. It wasn't long before she found her gaze fixed to a certain player again. She smiled and thought about the many changes taking place around her and inside her. It all seemed to snowball since Dave asked her to join the Leadership Team. "God is amazing," Lexi mused in celebration. Lexi knew without a doubt that He had put her on the Leadership Team to pull her out of her shell and help her develop confidence. He had allowed things to happen to her with the knowledge that it would shape her for service to Him. But through it all, He had protected her every move.

Observing the game without really watching it, Lexi poured out her love and thanks to God until boisterous cheers from Nick and Trent shattered her thoughts. She looked over at them and noticed they were on their feet and cheering Dylan as he calmly lined up a shot at goal. She jumped to her feet along with Hope and watched as he sent the ball sailing from forty-five meters out straight through the middle. The crowd erupted as the goal cemented the Tiger's Grand Final championship, and Lexi cheered alongside her friends. Watching Dylan and his teammates celebrate their inevitable win, Lexi's heart swelled with happiness for him. When Dylan looked over at them, and locked eyes with her, Lexi's body responded as she smiled back. She knew God wasn't finished with her yet. At this stage, He'd only let her glimpse the future He had planned for her. However, hindsight told her that if He brought her this far safely, then He would continue the work started in her and would carry it onto completion. Smiling as she retook her seat, Lexi wondered what the completed version of herself would be like when an unmistakable voice entered her thoughts: *'Trust me.'*

BIBLE STUDY

LEXI

1. In Chapter Four, Dave says to the new Leadership Team: *"It's a well-known fact that in difficult times we are refined and our strengths highlighted."* What does this sentence mean?

2. Whatever God raises up, Satan will try to bring down. List the way(s) this battle is demonstrated in Lexi's story.

3. We don't just ask and get. God grows us in the area where we are asking for help. How did God answer Lexi's prayer for confidence?

4. The Bible verse Dylan gives to Lexi before she makes her Uni presentation is found in 2 Timothy 1:7. Why do you think he gave her this verse. And was it the right verse at the right time?

5. Read Proverbs 11:14 and explain how this could have saved Lexi great heartache.

NOTE FROM THE AUTHOR

Youth Groups are common and operating in nearly every town and city. If you enjoyed Lexi's story and would like to be a part of a Youth Group, simply contact your local church and enquire when their Youth Group meets.

God Bless,
Karen

(Philippians 4: 6-7)

ABOUT THE AUTHOR

K.J. Rowe began her writing career in 2012 with the drafting of her Young Adult series called "Casts of Silver", The series, born out of her own unique experiences and understanding how books can literally change people's lives has been crafted to spotlight particular issues common amongst young people. To impress upon youth the importance of listening to their inner voice, remembering their self worth and to trust in Gods perfect plan for each of our lives is the mission and vision of this series. Karen lives with her husband and 2 children on a farm in North West Victoria, Australia.

www.ingramcontent.com/pod-product-compliance
Lightning Source LLC
Chambersburg PA
CBHW030323020726
47493CB00004B/1143